I0732329

To My Favorite Artist

Author: Darya Mohammadi

Translated by: Majid Karimi

Kidsocado Publishing House
Vancouver, Canada

Phone: +1 (833) 633 8654
WhatsApp: +1 (236) 333 7248
Email: info@kidsocado.com
https://kidsocadopublishinghouse.com
https://kphclub.com

Serial Number: P2346450130
Title: To My Favorite Artist
Author: Darya Mohammadi
Translator: Majid Karrimi
Cover Design: Mehrnia Nouri
ISBN: 978-1-990760-78-5
Metadata: Fiction / Drama/ psychology
Interior: KPH Design
Book: Paperback
Pages: 270
Canada Publish Date: January 2023
Publisher: Kidsocado Publishing House

All Rights Reserved, including the right of production
in whole or in part in any form.
Copyright @ 2023 By Kidsocado Publishing House
All Rights Reserved

Dedicated to Meaningful People

...

Contents

A few words with the audience:

Years ago, when I was a twelve-year-old, the idea of writing a novel called "In Search of My Lost Angel" came to me, but after a few weeks, I regretted continuing to write; Because I felt it was too early to write a good and effective book, which of course I was quite right.

Six years later, at the age of eighteen, I wanted to turn my writing exercises into a book, which included love letters to an imaginary lover, but that year I was mentally disturbed and had to give up everything because of my big entrance exam and focus on my studies; So, I still could not put my ideas into action.

I said this until I reached the spring of last year when most classrooms and centers were closed due to the covid 19 pandemic and home quarantines had begun. In those days, I was terrified of the news of death and illness. I was deeply homesick; I miss my relatives and friends, walking to college, after-class cafes, concerts with my favorite singers, watching new movies, no anxious hugs, and maskless meetings. I felt like I was in complete darkness. It is as if I have lost the meaning of my life. But one day as I was browsing my friend's posts in cyberspace, I came across the page of a spiritual guide. The first words I heard from dear professor "Faraz Ghorchian" were these sentences:

"Whatever happened in your life, ask yourself, how bad is this going to help me grow? What lesson does it want to teach me?! Believe me, all your wounds make sense. Just start walking in the dark."

His words were a flip to guide me back to the flow of life. From that day on, I made a new plan for my new lifestyle. I started reading books that I always liked to read. I learned a lot from great writers like Irvin David Yalom1[1], Wayne Walter Dyer[2], Mark Manson[3], Viktor Frankl[4], Helen Fisher[5] and Susan Anderson[6], and I felt love clearly in their books.

I took classes online with good teachers and continued my music practice, taking my lessons more seriously and

---

1 Irvin David Yalom: American psychiatrist, existentialist psychologist, and author.
2 Wayne Walter Dyer: American psychologist and motivational speaker, author of self-confidence books.
3 Mark Manson: American author
4 Viktor Frankl: Austrian psychiatrist, neurologist and creator of meaning therapy (logo therapy).
5 Helen Fisher: American anthropologist.
6 Susan Anderson: American author.

passing my classes with high grades. The idea of writing a book once again came to my mind, but this time more mature than before. In addition to music and poetry, I was very interested in psychology, so I decided to write a book in both literature and psychology.

At first, I was very scared and struggled with my perfectionism. I thought to myself that I would not be able to write until I had read those hundred volumes or ten more learning periods.

Once again, dear Master Ghorchian, whom I am always grateful for, encouraged me with his professionalism. I learned from their pragmatism to stop procrastination and not to expect perfect work, but to work on my goal continuously every day. It was I who dared to face my fear and try to write with all my heart and soul.

Introduction:

The book you have in hand is about a girl named **Delsa** who, on the night of her twenty-fourth birthday, rereads the letters she wrote to her lover Ryan during her treatment and remembers a time when she was struggling with a severe emotional crisis. She puts her feelings and emotions on paper to clear her mind of the toxins of the past.

The letters narrate the stages of mourning, memories, wishes, emotions and lessons that Delsa has learned from separation. By traveling inside, Delsa tried to get to know herself better, embrace her inner child, face her shadows and flaws, and create meaning for her life.

This book emphasizes that we must face our realities, wounds, and anxieties and not suppress our emotions, we must take responsibility for our own lives, love ourselves, and accept the facts of existence.

That no matter how much our loved ones are with us, there is still an inherent distance between us and the world around us. One day we will leave this planet, so we have to accept the quasi-deaths. The pen of our destiny is in our own hands; So, we have to take responsibility for our lives and pay the price for our choices. We also seek our own meaning in life so that we can continue to be committed to our lives and goals despite all the challenges and difficulties ahead.

Thanks to the good podcast of Mr. Farzin Ranjbar for analyzing the psychotherapy of existentialism[1] in the podcast with a simple and eloquent expression, With his explanations, good ideas came to my mind and changed the course of my story. In one of their episodes, he says:

"It seems that the only constant way to reduce existential anxiety is to focus on life itself. We should not delay living."

---

1 Psychotherapy of existentialism is a dynamic method that focuses on the existential anxieties of human beings and considers the root of all anxieties in the four basic fears of freedom, loneliness, emptiness and death.

I also decided to get rid of the fear of being judged and criticized and take advantage of the unique opportunity provided to me.

So, I wrote this book with the pen of my heart.

Thank you very much to my dear parents and kind friends who have always encouraged and supported me.

I am also very grateful to the dear editor of Ms. "Pardis Orizi" who helped me to improve my story with her good suggestions.

Now that I am twenty-three years old, I realize that the lost angel I have been searching for it for years is instilled in me.

This book was born as the most powerful meaning in the hard days of my life, and calmness replaced my worries, because the coronavirus gave me a chance to make my dream of many years come true.

June 2021

Good Luck and bye

Tonight, I will blow out the twenty-fourth candle of my life. Next week, I will perform for the last time in the F major group.

Although I'm deeply missed; I have to be strong and prepare for a new life.

I was picking up my clothes when I saw a box in which I had found the letters I had written to Ryan two years ago. I could not believe that two years had passed since those events. I remember very well the day Ryan left ...

As I played Chopin's 8Minor Waltz, my thoughts twisted like a chain around my mind, distracting me. I could not understand that amount of passion. Out of nostalgia, the pain had reached my bones.

With his warm voice, I wanted to pour clear water on all the pus of my annoyance and melt the ice of my nostalgia. So, I picked up my cell phone to call him, and suddenly, seeing his message, cold water poured down my whole being and thoughts. Not only with my eyes, but with every cell of my body, I stared at my phone screen.

He deleted his recent messages and sent a new one:

"Hello, dear Delsa! We will not have a class together anymore."

It was clear from the placement of the word "dear" next to my name that it must have no intimate tone.

I could not stop shaking my hands; With all the difficulty I typed:

"When did we become strangers together? What did you see in me but love and respect?"

He replied: "Have I ever disrespected you?"

I was afraid to say anything which make him more determined to go. I typed:

"No, you did not. But what happens? you replay my Instagram stories; Then you delete your messages one by one. Do you think this is normal?"

He answered: "Please transfer my money to my account. I'm waiting." It was a terrible shock. I did not know what to do.

I said: "I will not do this until I see you and talk to you."

And he replied: "OK. So, nothing."

His tone was so cold and icy that every word that came out of his mouth froze on the roof of my psyche. I said:

"If I said those words, I just wanted the annoyances to be forgotten. I thought you understood me. Well, I accept it; it was my fault. I became very emotional. The past is past. Forget it, Ryan. I have not given you your birthday present yet. We are still working together. Who said that your feelings are important to me and that I never wanted to hurt someone like you. Who said that I do not want to lose you in my life. what happened?"

He   replied:
"Give both to a needy person."

I said: "Stop it, Ryan! You know how emotionally disturbed I am. I need help more than ever. Please do not leave me alone in these difficult circumstances ... I miss you very much."

Ryan aimed the last bullet straight at my heart and fired: "Good Luck and bye ..."

The first letter

My dear Ryan!

I knew an angel from heaven whose name was Saturday.

His perfume cannot be found in any store. His fragrance wafted through the room and made my whole room fragrant. With the watercolor of his hands, he gave joy to the wall of my moments, and with the light of his gaze, he illuminated the ceiling of the night sky.

But there is no more news of that kind angel. It is as if he had been exiled to another land and left no trace of himself anywhere on the days of the week.

My moments, like a swamp of anger, have suffocated my laughter, and the lotus of hope has died, and now a black hole called Friday has swallowed my days, and darkness has taken over my whole world.

This is the first Saturday I do not see you, and from now on, all my days will be Friday evenings.

The second letter

My red fruit!

When I saw your name on the screen of my mobile phone, I could smell the delicate scent of strawberries.

I have read that strawberries reduce emotions such as fear, anger and anxiety, and they are good for eyesight and relieve fatigue.

When I saw you, the image of everything was engraved in my mind in the most beautiful way possible. When I saw you, I just found myself and my mind calmed down.

With the tremendous energy you gave me, the tiredness went away from me and I was so bold and reckless with you that the word fear had no meaning in the dictionary of my life.

Your presence has the warmth of a strawberry, and your words evoked a delicious taste.

My strawberry! For days now, in the house of my mind, I no longer smell the fragrance of tenderness.

The third letter

My dear Hardhearted!

You do not know, from the moment we separated and you blocked me from everywhere, I have gone through various suicide methods in my mind several thousand times.

I do not consider myself alive right now. I have no desire, no purpose, and no meaning to continue.

My life is long over. The only thing that has kept me going so far is a box with your beautiful photos, with a notebook of my songs that is a part of me and the azure dress that you said I would send you the photo.

I am looking for a way to deliver your gifts to you. Every night I endure the torment of opening my closet and finding myself in a situation where my tongue is stuck and I have nothing to say.

If someone asks me to explain the miserable situation I am in, I can say nothing. I do not know what all my insistence on delivering this box to you is for; When you did not have the slightest desire for it. Now that you have closed all communication channels to me!

How happy I was. In return for this work, I would like you to share the pleasure I caused myself, for a few moments. How I wanted to see the happiness up close and enjoy it. You even took this small request from me. You withheld this small wish and your sweet smile from me and left me with a thousand questions in my mind. I feel like my best friend has crushed me under his feet and passed me by train. How can I love and trust someone again?

Ryan! Give me the right not to be able to forgive you. What you did to me broke the vessel of my pride, feeling, confidence and self-esteem.

You domesticated me like a little prince and told yourself that it was her own fault, she wanted me to domesticate her; But you did not know the secret of the fox:

"You are responsible to the person you tame for as long as you live."

The fourth letter

My dear Ryan!

Where are you now? What are you doing? Who are you with? Do you still remember me? How simple it is to say: Forget the past and live in the present.

The past is a part of me that is crumpled like crumpled paper in the grip of memories. How do I untie the knots of my being?

I feel like a prisoner of great sorrow.

By writing, I try to take this great sorrow out of my being and free myself from its captivity. I want to line up all the wagons of memories in the train of my mind once again and bring them on the rails of paper lines. I think to myself, if I had not craved a cup of lemon tea that snowy Tuesday and gone to Pedal

Cafe, the same cafe where you played the music, I would be in a different situation now.

I remember that day very well. The soft light and the secluded and romantic atmosphere of the cafe gave life to the birth of new songs. I picked up the pen, and as I was thinking, the sound of your instrument caught my attention.

For a few minutes, I closed my eyes and listened indescribably to the song "Gone" by "Ali Zand Vakili" which was played by your artist's hands. I felt that after a long time my heart wanted to write:

"Clear this dust of sorrow from my tired pedal,

Open your notebook

On my broken body,

My whole being is wounded.

Tune all my feelings

By C D E note of music, that my injury is too much.

Put your feelings

In the music of your heart, Be my musician

Call me by musical notes."

I will never forget the good feeling of the moment when I was with you for the first time. It was as if a wave of joy hit the rock of my sorrows and the ship of peace anchored on the shore of my heart.

I wanted to tell you from the bottom of my heart that no pianist had ever attracted my attention like this; And I loved the feeling that was born in my heart from the sound of your instrument playing, very much. But everything just went through my mind. I left the cafe that day without any discussion.

On the way home I just realized that I had left something very important; My heart ...

The fifth letter

Dear Ryan!

Do you remember the day you asked me for cooperation and said that you would like to be more in touch?

My songs were the starting point of our relationship.

That day was also your birthday, and it was a special and important day in every way. I was glad to meet you at the beginning of flipping through a new page in the book of your life; But to be honest, I was scared of all this too much passion and I felt like I was overdoing it. I was constantly blaming myself and looking for a way to unload these intense feelings. I was afraid to lose control and say how much I was interested in you and excited to have you.

I gave my feelings a chance for a month. But not only did the flame of my passion not go out, but every day it was burning more and more and I felt so much fire inside me that I could not stop my cheeks from blushing and my heart from beating.

I was afraid one day you would find out who was sending you those anonymous love messages and we would lose contact. On the other hand, I felt distrustful of the people I met recently because of the failures I had experienced in the past, and early on, because of this, I hurt and upset you; Of course, I realized my mistake and apologized, but it was really hard for me to trust.

Every day the attraction of your voice draws me more to you and moves my feelings in the orbit of your love; Although I denied it in those days, I knew in my heart that I had a deep feeling for you. I used to say the words of my heart in my songs and I would send them to you under the pretext of cooperation. One day, in the midst of these songs, you started talking about the song I sent to you. This was the song,

"From now on, I will fall in love with your eyes,

I fall in love with the tone of your voice

and the sense of your beauty,

Reduce the curtain of these distances note by note"

You said:

"I will be dumbfounded by the music of your world."
"What a beautiful song Delsa! Who is the addressee?
For me?"

A voice in my heart whispered Forough's poem[1]:

"What lies within me is the sea,

When can I hide?

With you from this terrible storm,

I wish I could tell you."

I smiled and said calmly:

"It has no addressee. But it can be for you if you
want."

 You answered mischievously:

"I cannot say. You should say. You have to decide."

I took a few deep breaths and said calmly and firmly,

---

[1] Forugh Farrokhzad was an influential Iranian poet and film director. She was
a controversial modernist poet and an iconoclast, feminist author.

"I would like to get to know the addressee of my songs better."

"Well, let's get to know each other better. Come on."

I felt that after a long time, life had shown itself to me. I wanted to recklessly express my indescribable joy.

That night was one of the best nights of my life. My mood does not fit into any words; I was extremely excited to get to know and communicate more with you.

For you, until the morning, I had repeated the song "Always be with me - Mehdi Yarahi" and listened to the words of my heart.

Fatigue had fallen like an ominous shadow on my instrument and pen, and distrust and boredom had taken over my world. When you arrived, I was overwhelmed by the songs. I was born again through your eyes and I believed in my existence and my talents.

Your kindness turned into raindrops in my heart and washed my heart from alley to alley from past pollutions; The soul of the songwriter healed me from the wounds of emptiness and revived the desire to write in me.

The sixth letter

My dear!

How much fun I had when you described your daily life to me:

After breakfast, you would go to the gym, work out for ninety minutes, then take a shower, eat and go to the studio. Even at night, if you had time, you read books.

I have not forgotten the nights we talked until late in the morning. I remember a song from those nights that is very dear to me:

"We are both artists,

We are proud and full of emotion, These days we little by little,

We know each other.

I am the poet of your eyes; I fell in love with you.

Every word of my poem, I make with your eyes.

Your tone for me,

It is calm and musical.

Emotional music,

It builds every second.

We are both artists,

A world full of secrets, from the seam of a wall, we
make a window."

The seventh letter

My Ryan!

You who wanted to go, why didn't you take your memory with you?! I wish the day you left in a hurry, you would not leave your memories, or at least take the good ones with you.

I remember one night I was very upset about something and I felt very upset; I calmed down very, very much when I discussed the matter with you.

You said, "Don't be upset, Delsa! laugh."

With these words, I wanted to laugh not only at that issue but at all the other bitter events; Because after talking to you, no more grief could remain in my heart and cause me resentment.

That night, your kind tone plunged me into an ocean of excitement and joy, so that I no longer cared about anything. I even thanked that matter for making you say that beautiful sentence: "Delsa, laughs."

You had a performance the next day and you had to go to bed early, but I wanted to stay up with you till morning and talk.

I slept only two hours that night and I was very excited.

I was more excited than you and I arrived at the concert venue earlier than the rest of the audience. Just as I was waiting for the doors to open, I saw you coming out of a cafe next to the hall.

A deep sensation entered my lungs and made its way through my pulmonary vein to my left atrium; Then my mitral valve opened and my clear blood entered my left ventricle with that gentle feeling and finally reached all over my body through my aortic artery.

Every time you looked at me from the crowd and blinked, my heart beat faster and my feelings for you became more and more. I have no doubt that day, love was an element of fire that burned me in its pleasant flame. It was the first time in my life that I felt I liked someone who also liked me and all his attention was on me. A sense of beauty was exchanged between us; A warm and hearty feeling.

As you said goodbye to each other, you put your hand forward and said, "Thank you for coming, Delsa. You made me very happy."

Like someone who has reached a spring in the desert after seeing dozens of mirages, this was the first time I touched your hand and it was no longer a dream for me.

Then we went into the elevator together and you said, "Still upset?"

"No, not at all."

I wanted to hold you tightly and say: "Crazy, can I see you and be upset!"

I wish I could freeze you in the moment you stared at me so that you would see me alone forever and you would no longer meet any strangers ...

I wish I could sell a few hours of my future and go back to a few hours of May last year. I wish...

The eighth letter

My dear!

Today in the library of my mind, to relieve my pain, I picked up the book happy moments and flipped through its pages one by one.

I read the memory of a night when I felt like a dead lady from a high fever and muscle aches.

Minutes later, you revived me with your words, and my pain was like migratory birds migrating from my nest and going away.

Another night when we were both not well, we decided to send each other positive energy.

After touching your good feelings from a distance, I fell asleep full of goodness and full of love for you, and with your good night, I had a good night.

Dear! No one could express the word crazy with the elegance and beauty that you were expressing. When you called me crazy, I wanted to continue my madness more and love you madly.

When you remembered me, when you expressed concern, I was reassured that I lived and breathed in the heart of someone I loved.

I remember very well the first night you called me "baby". The night you were in the studio until late and I said, "hope you are well," and you replied very sweetly, "Thank you, baby."

From that night on, I wanted to hear "baby" only with the frequency of your voice.

Simple words that I used to hear from many people during the day, but you were always different. I even distinguished between the words my dear, my darling, and my baby.

When you used the word "my baby", I felt that you loved that moment more than any other.

I wish I was really dear to your heart ...

The ninth letter

My sweet impression!

At that time, the sunset before sunrise and the days got dark before dawn. I never understood the reason for all this haste.

Why do moments not want to pass now?

I still could not believe your departure from my life. Separation from you is the deepest wound in the world that burns my heart like molten lead.

In the vacuum of your presence, the scent of your voice wafts through the clothes of my memory and I go to the past. When I called your name several times and each time you answered in a sweet and loving tone: "My baby"; Words were erased from my mind and a sweet silence was established between us. And when you called my name, I was out of breath and my lungs were getting oxygen from your voice instead of air.

Thinking of you, is a fresh and fragrant tea that will never be forgotten. I drink the tea of your remembrance and my heart is refreshed again.

You forgot, but I well remember that on Tuesday night, around nine o'clock, you called and said, "May I see you tonight, even for a few minutes?" I could not leave the house at that hour of the night and see you, but that sentence encouraged me so much that I wanted to travel the path of your love at a speed of a thousand kilometers per hour.

I remember our conversation and review it in my mind you said: "We have a class from next week, baby."

"Yes, my Master."

"Do not tease me so much."

"I like..."

"My baby ... Delsa, when you call me in your house, can I answer: yes my baby,"

"No, you are crazy, it's impossible. Mom, dad, and my sister Dorsa are all at home. You have to behave like a master in front of them."

"They want it a lot. I say you better invite your neighbors to come and sit between us!"

As I laughed out loud, I felt my red blood cells transmit the calmness of your voice to my tissues and drive the anxiety out of my lungs.

There is still a beautiful picture of you sitting here in front of me and smiling at me. I sit next to you, kiss your smile, caress your gaze, hug your picture and call your name with love.

The tenth letter

My dear love!

How I miss the minutes you smiled and counted the lines under your eyes.

I miss the velvet earlobes, the pale pink lips that grew brighter with each sip of water, the white shoes that always shone with cleanliness, everything that was a part of you.

I deeply miss the moments when you sat behind the piano in your red shirt and improvised on the emotional chords you heard from your heart.

Why didn't I tell you how much more attractive you are in red?!

I wanted your playing to be repeated in my small room forever. At that time, for hours, my eyes were sewing themselves into your clothes, and until the moment of my death, they did not blink even for a moment, and again I was born from the perspective of the most beautiful sequence of my life, and I lived a moment of your presence for a thousand years.

My favorite music was the tone of your calm voice, which calmed my soul, tuned my heart, put the notes of the words together, and played the melody of the song "I love you." in my heart.

I am madly longing for that memorable and fragrant perfume whose fragrant scent stays on my fingers for hours and brightens the night.

My fingers were cold keys that you warmed with the hands of your musicians.

Now the instrument of my heart is unhappy, my soul is not at peace, and the coldness of your coldness burns my hands.

I wish you could just sit next to me for a few moments and understand a small point of my feelings.

The eleventh letter

My dear Ryan!

When seven months had passed since we met and we became more intimate, I still did not know where I was in your life, how important I was to you and what my share of your heart was. We did not have a teacher-student relationship; We did not treat each other like two normal friends, we did not have a relationship full of love and commitment either.

I had no idea what to call our relationship.

In the seven months that I met you, I left the key of my heart in your hands alone. You were the owner. You could use the key and enter whenever you want without permission.

I was so in love with you that I could no longer love any other man. My whole fear was that you would not love me as much as I love you.

Our multiplication table was changing and fluctuating every day. Sometimes your attention was multiplied in a thousand cells of my love and it made my heart feel a thousand times better and sometimes your indifference emptied my being.

My life was divided into two parts: the day I saw you and the days when I counted the moments to see you. When I saw you, moments of love and magic passed before my eyes. I would put my hand on your hand and you would caress it by moving your fingers.

Your kind looks, your sweet smiles after the end of each sentence, the touch of your hands and the unique feeling that was beyond imagination, made me need you more and more day by day.

Our words spin like a whirlwind in my mind:

"Ryan, tomorrow I will have surgery on my wisdom teeth. I am very scared."

You said: "Are you crazy? It's not scary ... don't worry, darling."

"Well, baby, I'll try."

To distract me you said: "You put your hand in my hand, naughty…"

I replied: "Well, you took my hand first."

"No, who said that ?!"

"I say."

"Ok. I did well."

I questioned you: "Do you talk to everyone like this? Do you hold everyone's hand?"

You laughed: "Of course, not."

I asked again: "Ryan! Let me ask you a question. Tell me the truth."

"Ok."

"Do you Love me?"

He said with a pause: "Do you love me, Delsa? Please say. Can you tell me how you feel?"

I regrated to ask that question and said "I cannot say that. I want to be sure first. Of course, now may not be the right time. We better sleep now. Say good night to warm my eyes."

"Well, we'll talk, for sure. Good night baby ... Delsa?"

"Yes?"

We ended our conversation with a kiss.

That night I tried to get rid of all the negative thoughts. I imagined you hugging me and cuddling my hair. My emotions in that imaginary image were as real and vivid as if I had lived it a thousand times. My whole being was full of oxytocin[1]. I liked to sleep and dream in my mind until morning.

Almost two more weeks passed, but we still did not talk about our relationship. I reargued and said:

"Ryan! Do you have time for me?"

You said, "Yes. I have."

"Well, then why don't we speak clearly?"

"What is in your mind, Delsa?"

I was silent for a moment in surprise, and as I swallowed my hatred, I said: "I want to know if it matters to you or not."

"Yeah. You're important."

"How much?"

---

[1] It is an oligopeptide and neurohypophysis hormone in mammals that is produced in the hypothalamus and stored in the posterior pituitary gland and plays a key role in romantic communication. (It is also known as the love hormone)

You said again that one day we should talk about it. That night my diary was soaked with the intensity of my tears. Every time I wanted to talk directly and clearly about how we felt, you would make excuses and postpone it to another day.

You had not answered my messages for several days. I was so upset that I felt like a big dagger had stuck in my heart. Your careless trauma had hit my head.

I had such a terrible headache that it was as if my brain was bleeding. Until you finally called and said:

"Delsa! Believe me, you are not the only one who I ignored. I was very upset physically and mentally and I am not getting better."

It was torturous for me that I did not know what you were suffering from. I could not bear to see you in a state of illness and discomfort. The volcano was about to erupt inside me.

You were the only one who, no matter how angry or upset I was with him, could still make my hell more than heaven with one sentence.

Your memory did not let me think of sleeping. I sent a message and asked about the situation. You were not very well.

You said that you know the solution to your problem but you cannot be comfortable, you had a series of requests from God that you wanted to reach sooner and you were suffering from impatience.

I reminded you how talented you are and that as long as you keep focusing on the things you do not have and you will stop and cannot use your full potential. Then I told you about my Thanksgiving booklet and my progress. That booklet helped me see better what I had and was more motivated to keep going.

We had a class together the next day. Your eyes had a lot to say. I was strangely communicating with your eyes. You made me look so sweet that day that I felt like the most special and beautiful creature in the world.

You called me immediately after our class and apologized for your recent late replies, and thanked me for trying to improve your mood with my words.

Finally, after days of grieving over your illness, I could laugh and relax.

I was proud of myself and I was extremely happy. I felt like I was born to make things better for you that day.

"Did my words really work?" I said excitedly.

"Can't you see how happy I am? Can you say something and not affect me?! You were really beautiful today!"

At that moment, my heart was caressed by the unique and unique delicate senses.

I really want to describe the feeling of that moment to you, but words are too small and powerless to describe that deep and extraordinary feeling. You flew me in the sky of happiness without the need for wings.

At the same time, we told each other to take care of ourselves; Then we laughed and repeated our loving words again.

I saw myself better that day. I fell in love with myself that day and remembered this quote from Alain de Botton[1]:

"Until no one has seen us, we do not exist; We cannot speak properly until someone listens to us; In a word, we are not completely alive, as long as we are loved."

---

1 Alain de Botton: Prominent Swiss-English writer and philosopher

The Twelfth Letter

My dear Ryan!

I am writing this letter to you in front of a river that we were sitting on previous September. It was four o'clock in the afternoon. An anxious melody was playing in my heart with a loud beat. It was me and you and the heavy silence that accompanied us on the path. Of the three of us, only silence spoke.

Sitting next to you at the shortest distance had led my soul to a galaxy beyond the Milky Way. As you squeezed my slender little fingers, I felt that my brain's Caudate nucleus[1] was more dopamine[2]-rich than ever.

---

[1] Caudate nucleus: One of the basal ganglia of the brain
[2] An important messenger in the brain

After all, you were the one who dared to silence the silence,

"Let's talk! You say first."

"It's hard for me to say," I said in a low, trembling voice.

"Well, then first I say Delsa. I'm a frank man and I want to be honest with you. I know you like me. I like you too; But I would rather live with my emotional partner. I work from morning till night; I want the person I love to be with me when I get home. Delsa, I am very lonely and you have many limitations."

Then you stepped forward a little and while cuddling me you said in a calm voice:

"Now what do you say we do? Do you think there is a way to cope with my situation? You can think about my words for a few days. Don't decide soon."

"I can live with you if I am your wife," I said

"I may be planning to do it in a few years, but now it is too soon for both of us. I have not had sex for several months and I cannot wait any longer."

I lowered my head and, trying not to cry, said,

"There are so many girls by your side. I know it's easy for you to easily forget me and go with someone else. You did not like me at all."

You gently put a kiss on my cheek and said,

"Don't say that anymore. You are a very good and successful girl; Only our lifestyle is different and I do not want to force you to do something. I do not love you but I like you very much. If I did not like you, I would not be here with you now. I could have cheated on you like other girls, but you were different from me."

I did not know if I should be happy or sad to hear such statements.

It was there that I realized the foundation of your relationship is built on sand; Superficial and less durable ...

I realized how different our priorities are and how different our needs and wants are from a relationship. I drowned all those annoying thoughts in waves of emotion because my heart wanted something else and did not want to destroy the imaginary image it had made of you.

I suddenly threw myself into the sea of your arms and shouted, "But I love you, Ryan. I want you."

I was so overwhelmed that I did not notice that I had wiped half of my lipstick with your white shirt. I was so embarrassed about this and did not know what to say. You pulled my cheeks tightly and said,

"What can I do for you, you're crazy! Thank God I had another shirt in the car."

Then we both laughed and stared into each other's eyes. In a few seconds, I had forgotten everything and I would not take my hand away from you for a moment.

We hugged each other again and you said:

"Delsa! I never had a serious relationship. I know that if we want to be closer to each other, we can no longer have this intimacy like before. We can go out together like two good friends again, text each other, call, and still be together if we needed each other and we were not feeling well. I do not want to lose you."

You were like the man I had dreamed of for a long time. It was the first time I felt like I had found him. How could I pass you by so easily?

"Is it so comfortable for you to be just two ordinary friends? Can you really?" I said with a bitter smile.

"Well ... not really. It's not easy for me. Because I like you too. We can be two people in life who like each other, but without commitment, which of course I know you will not accept."

"Of course, I do not accept."

"So, you mean to say goodbye to each other?"

At that moment, it was as if I had forgotten my mother tongue. As I shook your hand, I thought that if this was our last hug and last meeting, I have no doubt that my heart would have no motive to beat. What else does it mean for me to survive?!

You said in a calm and gentle tone:

"Close your eyes for a moment ..."

With my eyes closed, I slowly felt the warmth of your presence more. I could not believe that I was living the same novel scene that I imagined in my mind every night. As much as I knew the meaning of that bitter kiss, it was the best moment of my life. Because it touches the lips of someone I worshiped like crazy. I wanted the earth to get tired and dizzy from spinning around. Then sit quietly and carefree by the moon, drink freshly brewed tea and refresh your breath. Until that beautiful day arrives late at night so that I can stay in your arms more so that I can feel your perfume more on my hair and caress your hands on my face.

When I got home, my legs were locked in disability and they did not want to get off. "Call me at the same time in five years,"

you said with kind eyes as they chased me away.

"I would like to know how much you have changed and where you have reached."

I answered hesitantly "Certainly, I have not forgotten you, my dear, no matter what change I have made or wherever I have come! Now, before I go, I want to …"

You replied, "Okay baby! But this makes it harder for both of us!"

The end of the day was so bitter that I did not sleep for several consecutive nights and cried until dawn.

But I wish that was really the end of our story. I wish we could part with a kiss and good memories at the same point. If I had known that after that, everything would change and the end of our story would be bitter and sudden, I would never have insisted on continuing our relationship and I would not have given any chance.

I remembered a sentence I had read years ago in a book, The Opinions of a Clown.[1]

"One should never try to repeat moments. They should only be remembered as they once happened."

I want to remember from all your words only "I love you" that you said at once and forget the pain for a few minutes with the laughter that it brings to my lips.

---

1 The Clown (German: Ansichten eines Clowns, lit. "Views of a clown") is a 1963 novel by West German writer Heinrich Böll.

The thirteenth letter

My cherry blossoms!

Today I walked to the garden of my memories.

At the beginning of the path, it was snowing sweetly, reminiscent of the winter we met. A small snow piano stood by the white-clad trees and sang with the wind. A waterfall flowed from my eyes and reached the river of your love. The farther I went, I came across trees with fragrant cherry[1] blossoms and green apples. The red anthurium-shaped heart[2] flowers were reminiscent of the spring I fell in love with you.

---

1 Symbol of happiness
2 Symbol of strong love and emotions

The whole garden of my heart was full of white chrysanthemums[1] and pink orchids[2].

After passing a cool summer of your presence, I came to a cold winter that froze all the sea of my imagination.

I reached the dark part of the garden. Where I had planted the seedlings of our love and hoped that one day, they would bear fruit; But our world was so different that you could never fall in love with me. Eventually, my young seedlings tilted and rotted in the storm of rejection. Look at my little garden where all the seedlings of sorrow are bearing fruit today.

---

1 Symbol of honesty
2 Symbol of pure kindness

The fourteenth letter

A month has passed since you left ...

Today, when I saw the black page of your profile, I was so upset that it was as if a pile of coal had been sprinkled on the white canvas of my world.

How could I not write to you out of the sadness I feel in my heart? I feel like Albert Camus[1] who wrote in a letter to his beloved Maria:

"Today I was affected by the commotion and the rupture in which you are. Today, more than ever, I am ready to give my best so that I can kiss you with all my sorrow."

The sharpness of grief clings to the wall of my heart so much that it makes me call you; But I prefer to

---

[1] Albert Camus: French writer, journalist and philosopher.

ignore the feeling in my heart and share the grief remotely.

Perhaps the worst experience for a human being is the loss of a loved one.

I can understand you very well now, darling, because I am in bitter mourning.

Ending a relationship to which, all your emotions are tied is an experience no less than death.

Melancholy has left me bedridden for hours, paralyzed, and disabled. During the day, without doing anything, my energy is severely depleted and I get tired. I feel so empty as if I have buried my whole being with my lost loved one. The night is the killer of my sleep. The night injects me with pain and throws me into the depths of darkness. I want to sleep to lessen the pain of waking up; But every time I close my eyes, I see the images of your departure clearly, and I cry involuntarily in my sleep.

I also have a nervous tic; I keep shaking my legs and tearing the corners of my nails with my teeth. I do not want to eat food, because I am sad enough that you are not. I have lost so much weight that I look like a moving skeleton. I feel like my bones are going to melt every moment.

We are both mourners, except that no one recognizes my grief. You are still in this world and in the lives of your friends and loved ones and no one has lost you. This is my world where you no longer have a physical presence.

No condolences are held. No one comes to see me for condolences and sympathy, while each of my cells is mourning.

I feel discarded. I feel there was no difference between being or not being for someone. I am just pollen in front of this great world. Eventually one day I will not be even this little pollen anymore. When everything is going to be destroyed and forgotten, what difference does it make if I am or not? Do something or not. Why am I still alive? Why am I breathing? Why do I write letters to imaginary Ryan every day? Who am, I Ryan? Why am I? What am I doing here? Why should I continue? You will not return! My Ryan is gone!

The doctor says that I have to take Prozac[1] to get out of this situation. What can Prozac do? Can it change the past?

Do antidepressants give me meaning in life? Can they make you love me and not leave me anymore?!

---

[1] Brand of fluoxetine, an antidepressant

You yourself did not want me to be your companion during your hard days; Otherwise, I was present in some moments of today without any struggle. So, what kind of pain will my call relieve me of but remind me that it is not the desired subscriber in your world.

The fifteenth letter

My delusion!

Blessed are the spring clouds, which can rain and lightning. I am a snowball frozen in the unbearable cold of nostalgia that sheds its tears.

I could not have imagined that one day I would have to ask our mutual friend to deliver the gifts to you.

Thank you very much Sepehr for doing this. Of course, I kept your clothes to myself. As long as those are in front of me, the hope of your return breathes in my heart.

Today I feel worse than ever.

My wound is infected and emotional calluses have formed between me and the outside world.

Recognizing the border of a dream from the truth has become to me like a hair; So thin that I sometimes forget to suffocate half of my being in a sea of my fantasies.

I do not know what to do with all my unfulfilled regrets and dreams. I miss that night when you were not well and you wanted to walk on the Roof of Tehran together. I wish I could come with you and stay with you until morning. Or the night you played the piano in concert and you wanted me to be with you, but I was not in Tehran and I did not see you for three weeks, and all those three weeks I got sick from nostalgia, insomnia and hunger, and I went to the doctor.

My dear Ryan!

How I loved that once we tried the coffees of Viona Cafe in Ferdows Garden. Once we went to see that famous curly musician that we both loved and watched his performance up close.

The day you came to see me, I was making the most delicious lasagna in the world for you and you fell in love with my cooking. I wanted to stop with you for hours on the Haqqani Highway; I was looking at you lovely and I was passing heavy traffic with love.

One night in the back alleys of Darband, I would put my head on your shoulders and flip through my songbook.

I wish one day we would go to the Nature Bridge and then sit in front of the water and fire fountain and talk to each other with our eyes.

I would have liked to go shopping in the crowded Tajrish market to get more acquainted with your tastes.

I liked that at the highest point of Milad Tower, while the city table was spread under our feet, we looked at the murmur of silence, hugged each other tightly and promised to be together at the moment of our death.

I wish we went to the city theater together one night. You watched the show and I wondered how you looked.

After that, hand in hand, we walked in the rain-soaked streets of Valiasr and sang "Forough" loudly in the pleasant echo of the rain:

"Yes, it is the beginning of love, Although the end of the road is invisible, I do not think about the end anymore,

That love is beautiful."

Forget the past days; I miss the days that never came.

Nostalgic memories that never had a chance to be recorded in the mind. Nostalgic moments that died before birth.

The sixteenth letter

My artist!

Today, when I touched the keyboards, my heart was getting heavier and louder with hatred by playing the number two Nocturne[1] by Chopin's beloved composer.

Playing has become the hardest job in the world for me. I cannot sit behind my instrument and not remember the tragic moment of your departure.

I was reminded of my last year's performance of how stressed I was. When I called and shared my concerns with you, you said from the memory of your first performance on stage how stressed and scared you were.

---

[1] A piece of music based on a European tradition for playing at night.

Hearing your kind voice and encouragement, my heart calmed down and I decided to spend the rest of my time practicing. On the day of the performance, when I saw you, every cell of my body played an instrument of relaxation.

At that moment, I promised myself to give my best. Your presence was the best encouragement for me in the world. The moment I wanted to come on stage, you said to everyone, "Delsa is my artist!"

I did not fit in my skin at that moment.

Another great night was spent with you, and I was extremely happy that you thought I was able to perform so well.

Ryan my dear! My dear!

For three months now, I have been trying to wash and polish the spots of sorrow that have clogged the thin glass of my heart with my tears.

I have been following my doctor's advice for three months and writing down my feelings and memories. He says,

"It clears your mind of the toxins of the past and I gradually experience a sense of lightness and calm,"

He constantly insists that challenging emotions only prolong the grieving process. I have indeed come out of that initial and terrible shock over the past three months, but my inner homeless child is still screaming inside me and longing to be hugged. Your empty space that is all over me hurts ...

Everything has faded in front of my eyes and turned into the color of the night sky. The color of your eyes ... the color of your favorite.

Today, at this point, I am neither a colleague, nor a student, nor a friend; But I still have a small relationship with you ...

"I miss you."

I miss you so much that the vastness of the world of my heart can only fit you.

You are not here to watch my rehearsals, sing my songs and listen to my professional songs. You no longer tell me anything about your songs, your new collaborations, your anxiety and your worries. You will not send any more photos after the performance and you will not ask my opinion.

Tonight is my birthday night and I know very well that you will no longer send me to the clouds with the first congratulatory message.

The seventeenth letter

My dear!

Every time I talked to you; I felt the spirit of love return to my body. The false image of my mind was so powerful that I hid the face of truth under the guise of my imagination and could not see it properly although we talked, we could not be like two friends.

We continued our half-hearted relationship, and that was the beginning of the devastation. With your warm messages, you showed me a replica of paradise, and as soon as I wanted to believe in that imaginary paradise, you would disappear for a few nights and burn me in the hell of my anxieties and longings.

Talking to you was so enjoyable that it seemed to erase all my annoyances from my memory. But as soon as you ignore me again, my grief increased with all its might. Of course, I knew that you had not been physically and mentally well for some time; So, every day I prayed for your well-being and tried to understand you.

I will record our conversations in this letter so that they will not be forgotten. One night, with a bag full of apprehension and confusion, I sent a message to you:

"Ryan! Babe! You know very well that I always wanted to make you feel good and I always wanted to be a positive person, but sometimes I have the right to be sad and upset and tired.

You told me last week that you have severe anxiety; Work and financial problems are pressing on you, and I understand all of these issues, my dear, and I am willing to do whatever I can to solve them, but I feel that you are distancing yourself from me on other issues.

Ryan, I'm not feeling well. Because I do not know if the person, I am worried about is still worried about me or not. The person I love still loves me or not!

If for any reason you want to leave me tell me, and I will leave myself. Because I do not want to crush my character under the burden of love. But if that is not the case, I will try to understand you and help you again."

After two days, you replied to my message:

"Hello, my dear, may God bless you, I will not be able to see you today!"

I could not say anything at that moment because of the intensity of the sadness I felt in my heart. The next day, when I was a little better, I sent a message:

"I miss you so much, Ryan!"

"My dear. Are you well?"

"Yes, my love, are you okay?"

You did not answer ...

 "Ryan!" I continued:

"I have a question for you. Do you like to be alone when you are not well?"

He said, "Yes, usually."

"I wish you would tell me this."

"Excuse me, Delsa! Send me a photo to see you."

"Dorsa is asleep. I'm afraid to wake her up. Send a photo if you can."

"OK."

"Why don't your eyes smile at the picture?... I want everything to be right soon."

"It's gonna be OK. First, I have to be more patient."

"Ryan, should we go to the Roof tomorrow after class? Maybe we got better."

"I'll tell you, baby."

"OK. Let me know in both cases!"

"Okay, baby."

"Don't upset yourself, lest I grieve."

"Okay. you too. Take care of yourself."

"Baby, Take care."

Two days passed and I guess you did not call. I turned off my phone and cried like a spring cloud. I asked God to show me the way and save me from this swamp of death.

One day you would get warm and I would take a step forward, the next day you would get cold and I would take my steps more slowly. The same warm and cold as a hurricane had disturbed my psyche. I was trapped in a terrible purgatory and thought I had no way out.

My whole body ached and my muscles contracted. I was addicted like a cigarette and I knew how poisonous and deadly our relationship had become, but Acetylcholine[1] was no longer secreted by the brain and was calmed only by the nicotine of your voice. Maybe that's why the farther you went, the more I needed you, and damn it, this is the bitterest confession of my life.

When I turned on my phone, you sent a message without caring at all about what happened to me:

"Are you awake, darling?"

It's not like you froze me waiting. Every week you canceled our class under various pretexts and answered my calls occasionally.

I was so angry with you that I could not answer quickly. I decided to act like you once to see the pain of indifference!

As I guessed, you were upset that I had not answered for just a few hours. How did you expect me to endure behavior that you could not bear for a moment?

---

[1] Acetylcholine: The first neurotransmitter

Unable to bear the inconvenience, I called and apologized on your behalf, saying that we should see each other next week.

You also said, "Okay, Baby. Sure."

The taste of your love was blurred in the mirror of our relationship. The sharp smell of your departure could be heard in the distance, and every moment I tasted the bitter sound of footsteps moving away from me. You had purely disturbed my five senses.

I called again and again to pick up that damn phone: "Yes, Delsa! Yes?"

"Ryan? So where are you? When will you arrive?"

"I am not in Tehran."

"What?! So why didn't you tell me two days ago when we talked?"

"Well, today, when I did not answer, you should have understood it."

"You mean you shouldn't have given me the news? You did not answer me for two days!"

"Well, I was always busy with my work and my class. So why are you calling so much? Do you have anything to do?"

"Ryan?! ..."

"Please. Goodbye."

Moments later, from behind the phone, Sol-Dies' black note was repeated in a rhythm of two or four, and a sad musician in my throat played my sobs.

The feeling of anger was pounding like rusty nails in my head, my legs were shaking, my teeth were clenching, and my hatred was so heavy that it was as if I had swallowed a large rock. Was this two-headed giant the same prince I wished for from God every night? How strange I found you at that moment. You were not the one I met the first day. On which day of the calendar did the person I loved suddenly pack his baggage?

Four deadly weeks have passed. The air was getting colder. The wind combed the tops of the trees and the leaves fell one by one and were crushed under the feet of passers-by. The black clouds of November rained down and washed my tears with theirs. However, according to the time of the planet Earth, one month had passed since your departure; But a century had passed since the time of my heart. I was so overwhelmed with grief and my appetite was almost blinded. Every time I tried to sleep; a short film of your kisses would be displayed on the screen in my mind. I woke up with palpitation and intense stress, with a cold sweat, I put my head on my wake pillow and watched the wall of my grief until morning. I had a terrible sore throat and flu. I had a fever and a headache; you post your photos on Instagram by the beach and the sea every day.

I had completely forgotten the world before you. I had forgotten that I laughed before you, I sang, I wrote poetry, I sang "Forough", I lived before you. But anyone who tried to remind me of this, in my opinion, was only chewing on useless sentences. Someone who has lost her memory in a love affair has a hard time remembering before. I just wanted you back. It did not matter what you brought to me. I could not stand more distances. I had endured a month full of pain, stress and illness, hoping for your return.

Really Ryan! Do you remember what other date you did not miss?

"I want to know the date of my death!"

The eighteenth letter

My dear hearthstone!

I remember that rainy Tuesday evening. After a month away, your beautiful name was on the screen of my phone again! Unbelievably, as if a great miracle had happened, I stared at the message you had given for a few minutes and could not even utter a word.

I knew this image did not fit me at all, but in the words of *Susan Anderson*: "Quitting love is like quitting heroin."

I had become so addicted and found myself alone and helpless in the face of your love that I could not take responsibility for ending this poisonous relationship myself.

I called you while all my bones were shaking from the cold and anxiety. You finally removed my number from the list of annoyances! The sound of the last time we talked was constantly ringing in my ears, and the image of my feelings for that day, in the costume of an angry and depressed soldier, paraded before my eyes.

With the fifth horn, you picked up the phone and this time greeted me warmly and asked how I was.

"Thank you, Ryan. I am fine."

I did not make the slightest mention of what had happened to me. Just as the night could not coincide with the day, all my annoyances and sorrows could not be expressed by hearing your voice. All my pain was breathing until I heard your voice in the room of my heart. Your voice took the breath away from my sorrows and suffocated them. But an emotion inside me shouted my name and asked me to say something:

"Ryan, I was very upset the day you hung up. Your work was not right, baby."

"You were calling too many times."

"Because you should have informed me that you were not coming. A message would not take you more than a few seconds ..."

"Very well. Did you notice that the piano performance was delayed for two weeks? Are you coming?"

"Yeah. I am ... Ryan! Do you still remember what I said?"

"Delsa, I really wanted to; But I saw this way, I cannot continue with these conditions. I'm in a relationship with someone right now. She will be upset if she finds out. We can only be two ordinary friends. Two good friends ..."

Silent hands held my mouth tightly for a few seconds; So I felt suffocated. I cleared my throat and said with artificial laughter:

Silent hands held my mouth tightly for a few seconds; So that I felt suffocated. I cleared my throat and said with artificial laughter:

"Wow! Congratulations! Congratulations very much. When did you buy the sweets?"

"I have to give you dates, of course."

"Yeah. Bring me Halva, too. Don't forget!"

"How are you, Delsa?"

"Me? Yes, I'm. I'm perfect. I'm very well. I'm so happy. Very much ..."

"Well, Delsa. See you. Do not forget your exercises. Take care. goodbye."

"..."

A sad incident in front of my eyes. This is my share when it's all over, I'm fighting with all my memories,

Hatred in my throat, I'm standing on a thousand mines.

The nineteenth letter

My dear!

I will not forget the night we had a class together again after a month. I wrote you a letter. I thought if I wrote you about my feelings, everything would be fine.

I must have guessed that you might have met someone during this time; Although I was acquainted with one of your friends, I had no intention of this acquaintance and there was no feeling.

Maybe I wanted to stimulate you. I was so upset at the time that I was ready to go out with any man for a few minutes of forgetfulness. When you understood this, you said that now we were equal. But what you did to me was very different from what I did. You stared into my eyes as you spoke and then smiled. From the same smiles that your eyes smiled with your lips. The ones I enjoyed and the sugar melted in my heart. I said in my heart that really, why does he not see so much love?!

That volume of my feelings did not fit in the small cup of your understanding, my dear. I remember that night after we said goodbye, I cried so much that sleep forced me to close my eyes. You indeed said your wishes about a relationship and it was I, who insisted that we have an emotional relationship while I am in Iran, but you also accepted. After that, you took back your words and pretended that you did not say such a thing at all. You told me that I should have known from your behavior that you withdrew and that you should not say everything.

Two weeks passed. I was very happy when I realized that there is no one in your life. I did not sleep at night thinking that someone else would touch you. I missed you, even when you were sitting in front of me.

I made chamomile tea for you. You looked at me and said:

"You spilled something in this; drink and die, I will get rid of you."

"Clever! how did you know?"

Ryan! This was not fair. You were so sweet that night. I just realized how much I love you. I could not lose you. I was angry with you, but I could not stay angry when I saw your nice face.

Friends, blame me for giving you my heart,

I must first tell you why you are so good.

Candles must be taken out of this house and blown.

It does not tell your neighbor that you are in our house,

 I told you to come and tell you my sorrow,

what can I say to make the sadness go away because you come,

Love and hardship, sorrow and blame,

It's all easy not to bear the burden of separation.

See how beautifully Mr. Saadi has touched my heart!

From that moment on, I gave our relationship another chance. I hugged you tightly and once again solved all my small and big annoyances in your peaceful Ocean. But this hug again, had a heavy price ...

I was hopeful when you said you were thinking about our relationship too. I thought everything was different this time. But the only days we had a class together were all good. We did not say anything special during the week. You answered my messages from time to time, and when I expressed my displeasure, you did not care and kept repeating them.

In those days my appetite was very aroused. I was trying to satisfy my emotional hunger with chocolate chip cookies. It is very difficult for your love to remain unanswered, but it is even more difficult to sometimes warm yourself with the attention of your lover and sometimes to light a candle in his careless ice.

Waiting or forgetting is deeply painful, but being trapped for a moment and not knowing you have to wait or forget is more painful. Out of great sadness, I cut my hair short and said to myself, what difference does it make if I have short or long hair?!

On the day of our class, you looked at me with surprise and frown; As if you wanted to protest. You would be attractive even by frowning!

"Is something wrong?" I said sadly.

"Don't speak. I'm angry with you."

"Why? Which of my words upset you?"

"You cut your hair short. You did not tell me anything you wanted to cut short. You knew I did not like it. But you did it."

"I did not think it would matter to you anymore. Everyone just says it's cute."

"Are you cute? Not at all. It takes a year now for your beautiful hair to grow back."

A few moments later, Dorsa entered the room and brought us a chamomile drink. When she closed the door, you looked at me and said,

"Why didn't you make it for me?"

"How about that?" I said in surprise.

You said in a calm and usual tone: "Oh, it tastes better when it is made by your hands."

Although I was seemingly silent, I had a thousand unanswered questions in my heart that I had to ask. That night, I temporarily took off my mourning clothes and had a small party for him.

Ryan! I thought you must love me when you say that. I did not know that the day will come when I say you loved me at all or not, you can easily say that I only liked you, that's it!

By the way, now that I am writing this letter to you,
I have a cup of chamomile tea on my table. You are
not here and it is not necessary to fight with Dorsa
for making it. My hair has grown much longer since
we last saw each other. But you are no longer to see

....

I am left in a world without spectators.

The twentieth letter

Still, tears well up in my eyes as I listen to your latest voice messages. Where did you target my heart so that it does not get better? It's as if my emotional bleeding is not going to stop.

I have written your word in my diary. I read them more than a hundred times:

"Hey Baby. I do not know where to start, or how to say it right now. From these clichés that everyone says, with the difference that I do not say. I leave the truth or falsehood to you. Pick whatever you like.

You are a really good girl. You are a poet, and a musician, you have a beautiful voice, and in general, I must say that you are a successful person. I really enjoy it. Most importantly, I think you can be a great companion for a man, but Delsa there are obstacles that cannot be forgotten.

My lifestyle is very different from yours. I do not want to make any judgments and say that your condition is bad and mine is good; Not at all. Everyone has their own condition. Call it whatever you like. Wenching, white marriage ... I do not know ... but I'm so comfortable.

If you were an ordinary girl, I would not tell you this. I was playing with your emotions. Finally, I could cheat on you once, abuse you, and then leave you. But I did not. I did not because I said you are a good girl you deserve more. I should not play with your emotions. That's why I pulled aside.

Now, you may think that I am very relaxed and comfortable, I will say these things to you, but believe me, I am upset from the inside. Because you could be a really good partner, although when I want to get married, that's not my intention; But I do not want to lose you as a friend in my life. I know how you feel. I know your kindness. I know you are kind to me. You are very good and I do not want to upset a person like you at all.

I know it is selfish, but I want you to still have me in your heart, even if you left Iran and entered into a relationship with someone. Love me.

That's it. Sorry, I took your time. Good night."

I always hoped that one day your decision would change and I would become the love of your life.

I could never get rid of the filth of your love as long as we were in a relationship. Even the day you said our world is different. Nothing changed. Neither my feelings nor your mischief.

You knew exactly where my heart was in charge of my feelings. You put your hand on the exact spot and pulled the toggle.

I had to cross my red lines to be who you want to be; But no matter how much I struggled with myself, I could not. It made worthlessness take root in me and I felt like my real self, the person I love, was running away from me. The day I set out with you to give you your birthday present, you did not answer any of my calls or messages for hours. My hope, of which only a small bud remained, waits for a message from you waiting for spring. When I shared my feelings with you so that there would be no ambiguity, you said with a laugh that it was a lesson so that I would not date you anymore. With this trick, you made my condition worse and sprinkled more salt on my wound. I felt like a failure. My heart is not broken; it was torn to pieces. It got on fire. It was reduced to ashes.

Your disrespect made me punish and blame myself. I blame myself for everything. It made me think I'm not good enough, I'm not lovable enough, and I'm right about that. I will never forgive you. Never...

You sometimes hear my voice messages. Without saying goodbye, you would leave my chat page and open my messages a few days later, but you would not apologize at all for your annoying behavior, and you would be upset if I did this to you.

You were no longer even with me as a friend.

But you did not teach the song that I wanted to cover for my friend because, as you said, you did not want to be in the heart of my social boyfriend....

And again, you wanted me to make the tea for you myself, to make it more delicious ... You just wanted me to love you, without intending to do so yourself.

You yourself confessed to being selfish.

Without taking responsibility for your behavior, you simply said that we did not have a relationship that you are now condemning me for. You said that we only gave each other a chance for a while. That's it Giving another chance only made me feel more and how calmly you said in response to my words that you do not think this is no longer my fault and it has nothing to do with me! ...

I thought I was definitely important to you when you were sensitive to my social friends.

In front of me, you praised other women and said that there is nothing higher than arousing female jealousy. What was the use of arousing my jealousy and touching on my weaknesses?

Maybe in this way, you were charging your sense of pride, selfishness and narcissism.

Maybe you enjoy arousing my doubts and emotional desires and keeping me in your state of desire.

Playing with someone's feelings does not just mean making a promise to her and then deceiving her. You knew how I felt, but sometimes you showed behaviors that made me hope again. You did not want to be with me, nor did you want me to leave you. You did not love me deeply and did not allow me to love anyone else. Whenever you wished or had the time, you would come to me and disappear again for a few days.

People's hearts are not dolls to play with.

We are responsible for the seeds of emotion that we sow in the garden of our hearts. I do not mean to say that you did it on purpose, but that was what I was faced with.

I could no longer bear the intense fever of my soul. I was tired; You stare at me with emotion every time you see me, but you do not answer my calls when you walk away from me. I was tired of your absurd talk and your unrealistic and selfish justifications that you were just trying to get me involved in loving you, without wanting to be myself. I was tired of you always resisting your mistakes and never admitting them. I was tired of constantly turning the lights of attention on and off and only looking at me in your spare time, not in my nostalgia ....

There is a huge and violent war going on in my mind.

I feel that this trauma is so deep that it has infected all my old wounds.

I thought I had forgotten them; But it was as if I had only soothed my pain for a while with the painkiller of your presence and handed it over to my subconscious. The wounds of rejection have piled up.

Perhaps one of the reasons I could not cut myself off from you was the fear of facing my old repressed feelings.

I feel like the old wounds have infected and no more painkillers will work.

The twenty-first letter.

Dear Ryan!

It's been six months, and you have left. All these six months, I was constantly in a whirlpool of denial, bargaining, anger, depression, and acceptance.

Although I became much lighter after venting my emotions, my anger and hatred manifested in the form of emotional and destructive attacks, which made me very sensitive and irritable. The slightest argument brings tears to my eyes. I am aggressive towards everyone and I get very angry; But I try to control myself and use the energy of my anger for positive things that work for me.

I have to admit that rejection is a very bitter and sad experience that has stimulated my body's defense system, reactivated old emotional memories, and made my need for you even more painful!

It is true that I cannot change the bitter events of the past, but I can accept it and feel the pain with all my being, touch its sorrow and grieve for this loss. Maybe this is the first time I can live fully in the moment.

So, I decided to think about my older memories. Memories that I was not willing to think about at all; But in order to achieve peace, I had to put down my old repressed feelings on paper.

Dariush was my high school chemistry teacher. With his encouragement, I became the first student in the class. I have always loved being the center of attention and he was the one who satisfied my need. I felt strong and special with him. He was one of my motivations for being accepted to the University of Tehran. Although I was not interested in pharmacy, I wanted to study it to win his heart.

I attracted a lot of students to his private conferences and classes. I edited and typed his channel content, and introduced his pamphlets, and in short, I benefited a lot. But the day after the entrance exam, everything I called, and he did not answer.

Suddenly I was shattered from within and the palace of my imagination collapsed on my head. I did not expect such behavior from him at all.

Two months later, I was accepted to the University of Tehran for Microbiology. I was so excited that the bitter events of the past no longer mattered to me. In that new environment, I wanted to start all over again and find my true love. On the second day of university, I met Soheil at the head of general physics class; A muffler boy with big honey eyes. He had a strong resemblance to one of my favorite childhood singers as well as my chemistry teacher. I did not know in those days that my subconscious is looking for people like my past to make up for its failures and continue its dreams with a replacement. When Soheil realized that I loved him, he became cold and heartless towards me and said that he loved someone else. We were in touch for the first few months of college, but he did not treat me well at all. He disagreed with me on all issues and we had nothing in common. The more I felt for him, the further he got away from me. I thought I had to be like him to make him interested in me. That's why I pretended to be rational and insensitive, hated traveling and hiking, and preferred to stay at home. I love solving physics and math problems, I listen to rap songs and I have no interest in literature and classical music. I had pursued all my interests so that Soheil would love me while none of this was the profession of my heart. I did not want to admit that he was not the right person for me. I was not interested in Soheil at all, but I was in love with a statue of Soheil that was built in my mind. Toward the end of the second semester, he told me that he was tired of paying too much attention to him and that he no longer wanted to be friends. A cascade of hatred had poured into the river of my mind. I was about to be failed that semester, I even thought of dropping out of university.

Until one of my college students, who was in my final year, shared his feelings with me honestly. My acquaintance with Roozbeh happened at the best possible time. When I was collecting pieces of my being ...

Roozbeh came into my life to say, as I am, it is very good and I'm lovable and I do not need to pretend to be what I am not. He fully accepted me. He made time for me. He paid constant attention to me and had a lot of respect for me. I felt very comfortable with him but with all this, I do not know why I had no special interest in him!

It was as if I was used to waiting to love others and begging for love from them!

I always behaved in such a way that I am not at all sure that this relationship will continue.

I was looking for something unattainable, but as soon as I got it, I did not want it anymore. Maybe I was suffering from an inner sense of worthlessness. Although I did not speak up and thought I loved myself very much, I did not make peace with myself from within.

Roozbeh had high self-esteem. He did not want to degrade himself and doubt his worth by my wrongdoings; That's why he left my life forever without asking for an explanation. He left nothing but good in my mind and I am very sorry that I upset him. I hope he forgave me ...

After that, I did not think I could love anyone from the bottom of my heart. I was tired of everything. I was not bored anymore. I was distrustful and pessimistic about everyone, but a few months later, when I did not expect it at all, I entered a new chapter in my life book.

One winter day ... Tuesday ....

Five in the afternoon ... Pedal Cafe ......

Lemon tea ....

Old piano and your artist's hands ....

This time, love appeared in the clothes of a pianist.

From my diary - Conversations with my inner child

"Hello, little Delsa. are you alright? I want to talk to you." "..."

"Please say something. I know you're angry with me. You have a right. I never talked to you. I always denied you. I thought talking to myself was stupid and psychedelic. I'm very sorry that I ignored your feelings and did not pay attention to you."

"I'm angry with you, Delsa. I'm very angry. You never believed I existed. Ryan loved me. You made Ryan go. He was very good. Very..."

"Little Delsa! my dear! Ryan did not want us. We cannot force people to love us. He was one like the others. One day he had to come to teach us lessons, one day he had to go. All these people come and go in our lives, Ryan was not supposed to be with us always."

"No! Ryan was different. The feeling I had for Ryan, I had no one else. I had never experienced this feeling with anyone else. He was my favorite creature on the planet. I feel my world is empty since he left. I miss that beautiful feeling so much. What if I never experience it again? What if I can no longer love someone?"

"My dear! Every person who comes into our life has a mission. He fulfilled his mission in our lives and left. Nothing can be done by begging and crying. Although it is very difficult, we have to accept the reality.

Remember the last time you sent him a voice for 30 minutes and cried? You wanted to let him know how much you were bothered and how much you loved him. But what did he do? It made your condition worse. He got further away.

As usual, I only knew how to suppress you. I deleted the last messages. Then I pretended that I no longer had a feeling for him and wanted to be just two friends. I am really sorry. Forgive me. I did not do the right thing. I had to tell him honestly that I was being harassed and that I could not continue the feeling that the fire was burning inside me every day. I should have asked him to go, but I did not dare. Because I did not want to face you. I just wanted to silence you and not take responsibility for my feelings.

Finally, Ryan escaped and left; But this separation was in our favor, baby. He had to go because you were so annoyed. Every time we gave him a chance, he disappointed us more.

Remember the night you did not sleep because of him. The days when you waited for messages to be answered but it didn't matter to him. When he hung up and then did not apologize. The day when you wanted to see him with all your love and give him a gift, but he could not even tell you that he could not come and you waited for hours. Remember all the times you were in a bad mood and crying because of him, baby.

You need attention, support and care, and most importantly, you deserve to be understood and accepted. He did not accept you. He wanted someone else. Someone who was not like us at all."

"Maybe I was not good enough that Ryan did not fall in love with me. I have not been able to attract anyone's love and loyalty so far. I'm not lovely. I have no value."

"No, no, not at all. You are gorgeous, kind, lovely and unique. You did not deserve to be rejected or abused at all. This was not your right. It's all my fault. I made you doubt your ideal. I did not love you enough that you became attached to the wrong people. Because of my carelessness, a trap of worthlessness and rejection has formed in your being, and you have always called on people in life to charge the expression of these traps. That's why I reject people who do not play games and

want to be with me. Because you are the one inside me. You did not receive enough love and attention from me that you wanted to receive love and attention from others."

"I always wanted you to see me. I was still not enough for you no matter how successful I was. You were still looking for other things. You always compared me to others. No matter how hard I tried, you still would not see me."

"I'm sorry, little Delsa. I should not compare you with others. I should not have blamed you. I was very perfectionist. From now on, I promise to reward myself for every positive thing I do for my goals to thank you. I pay more attention to my sleep and rest so that I do not get so tired. I promise to be careful and talk to you every day. If I were by your side, you would no longer have unhealthy attachments to people. I love you unconditionally as you are."

"How I wish someone would tell me this sentence now."

"From now on, you are going to hear this sentence from my tongue every day. I love you from the bottom of my heart, my sweet girl!"

"This sentence is the most beautiful sentence in the world. Thank you. I have always loved you and I wanted you to love me, too. I achieved my dream today."

"My dear. I hope you have forgiven me. Forgive me for all the days I have been away from you to be close to someone else. I promise not to sell you to anyone or anything. I am always with you; Because you are worth it. Now tell me how you feel now. What would you like us to do?"

"I'm so tired now. I am sleepy. I would like you to sing me a lullaby so I can sleep."

"Of course, my girl. close your eyes. Do not think about anything. I'm always by your side."

The twenty-second letter

My old friend!

I have been alone for a long time, examining my life and struggling with the thought that I am not worthwhile. I have just realized the importance of talking to my inner child.

Last night I talked to my little girl, part of my subconscious, and sang a lullaby to her. For the first time, I hugged my injured child and listened to her pain.

I imagined it outside of myself and put our conversations on paper. I tried to discover her most basic needs and desires. I realized how much she needs attention and care, and I, as an adult, have to take responsibility for and love my inner child. By doing this, I can help myself, become stronger.

I try to follow the recommendations of Dr. Shahrbanoo Ghahari[1] in her book "Ninety-Nine Ways to Heal an Inner Child".

To meet him, I wrote down my feelings every day and wrote him a letter. I do not stop crying when I feel bad. I say "no" where necessary. I laugh from the bottom of my heart and let my inner child appear. Whenever I am angry, I express her in words. I treat myself kindlier. I do not blame myself anymore. I decorate my room to my liking. I dress and make up according to my own taste. I take pictures of myself and capture my moments with my camera. I spend time with people I enjoy being with so that my inner child is more relaxed. I go to nature. I take a sunbath. I sit and watch the sunset. I write down my dreams and review them every night. I take out my long-forgotten Thanksgiving notebook from my desk drawer, make a list of all the things I am thankful for, and write down the good things of that day in that valuable notebook. I will expect as much as I can from myself and I will not put pressure on my inner child with high expectations. I rest myself during the day. I go for a walk, turn on the recurrence every day, and exercise regularly to increase my body's levels of the hormones serotonin and endorphins.[2]

---

[1] PhD in Clinical Psychology and Faculty Member of Iran University
[2] Natural painkiller whose main effect is pain relief.

My wounds are healing but they are very sensitive; I am careful not to get infected at all times and I am constantly taking care of my new emerging self.

The twenty-third letter

I feel that after many years I have lifted a heavy burden from my shoulders and emptied the trash of my mind; Although I struggle with the toxins in my wound every day and continue to suffer from the burning and constant pain, and rejection, in all its bitterness, was a great blessing to me. It helped me find a way to the wounds of my past and to learn the lessons I had already learned. It is true that I cannot change the bitter events of my life, but because of the lessons I have learned from them, I can consider them an opportunity for my own growth.

I raised your power and position to justify my crushing. It was my duty to come out from under this mental torture and save myself; But I stayed and endured the torture because I saw the victim's place as safer. Because I was afraid of the future. Because I was miles away from myself.

I realized that as long as I begged for love and attention from others, I would find myself worthless and unattractive to them.

I was attracted to people who made me feel like I was not good enough. The more they ignored me, the more I tried to get their attention, and eventually, they left me. This happened several times until I finally discovered a pattern; That I am afraid of losing.

The trap of release raises my adrenaline so much and mixes it with love that I can no longer distinguish between love and attachment. I was not in the vibration of love!

This extreme attachment and fear of being rejected made people feel completely confident and emotionally in control of me; So that I can be their emotional slave.

I'm not sure they did this consciously and intentionally, but they used my fear of rejection to control me, and I was the one who always said nothing and ignored it. I was the one who allowed them to do such things.

Do you remember our last words? The same night I sent you a 30-minute audio file and I cried! I still hoped you could understand me after hearing it, but things got worse. When I saw that you could not see and understand me from my point of view, I deleted our recent messages and took back all my worries so that you would not be upset. I never wanted to lie to you, but the fear of losing you made me pretend I could keep our friendship without any emotion.

That same day, my soul became angry with me. Because I tried to keep you in my life by force at the cost of losing myself. Every time I was not honest with my feelings, I betrayed myself a lot.

I had left earlier than you, but without realizing it, my wounded inner child was still insisting on your staying. Every day you clung to the wall of my heart and shouted your name loudly and threw the big stone of your presence right on the way of forgetting you. He never accepted the concept of the end, constantly putting together images of our good memories and passing them before my eyes in the form of a film.

I can still want you and love you. But what does it matter to love and want you when you do not want me? If I were important to you, you would be here now, asking me how I was and finding an excuse to stay! So, I have no right to be isolated and grieve for someone who, like a stranger, cut off contact with me and left.

Not everyone's past is always related to himself. Because you have had many relationships in the past, part of your being may still be involved in past issues and events. We can only touch someone's soul and have a good and healthy relationship if we allow ourselves to mourn and accept the sorrows of the past. That's when we can enter into a new relationship with all our beings. According to you, there were many who did not have any of my limitations and red lines, but each of them left their lives after a short time for their own reasons. So, if I had all the conditions to be with you, there would probably be other issues that would separate us sooner or later; Because our desires and expectations of a relationship were different.

It is good to live in the moment, but the future is shaped by our today's choices.

Some choices may harm our bodies and soul. Maybe what we choose today for our pleasure and excitement will cause us pain and suffering tomorrow and take us away from our original and good life.

I am no longer worried about depriving myself of the possibility of your return by saying the words of my heart or by doing something. It is time to overthrow your power and bring it back to me.

I need to be able to stand on my own two feet and heal my injured self. I should not look for someone who does not respond well to my feelings.

I deserve love, attention and respect.

Now that I understand my true needs, I find it unlikely that I will be attracted to someone with behaviors like yours.

I know that there are kind, committed and sensitive men on this planet. I'm looking for someone who has common goals; I do not want anyone who is not sure about being with me and part of his being to reject me.

I do not want anyone who does not respond to my messages for days and bury me in a host of priorities. My heart does not deserve disrespect. The person I do not care about does not matter to me and I will not struggle to stay. I do not need someone who does not apologize for his mistakes, I do not need someone whose values do not agree with mine and who does not want to be my companion.

Now that I know what I want from a relationship, I do not see myself as a victim and I do not think that family, culture, society, and dozens of other external factors have separated me from you.

I have learned from Dr. Azardokht Mofidi[1] in the book "Love and Psychoanalytic Analysis":

"No healthy person can love another person under any circumstances. A healthy relationship is a fifty-fifty, and one has to signal to love and receive the signal to be loved."

One person is not going to take on the heavy responsibilities of two people. Love would be a sweet illusion if we were both delusional.

---

[1] Iranian physician and psychoanalyst.

The twenty-fourth letter

My dear!

My situation today is indescribable. I will never forget what I saw. Even its image will not be erased from my mind for a moment.

It was six forty-five in the afternoon. I went to Cafe Viona with Hiva. I wanted her to be by my side and just listen to what I had to say. She was holding my hands and trying to calm me down. We were waiting for our coffee, which suddenly dried up when we saw you. How handsome you were! More attractive than ever. You were wearing a nice white shirt and red shoes. Your white glasses were over your head. I could not believe seeing you there. Oh! How I missed talking to you. A few minutes later, a girl of medium height, with long brown hair and black eyes arrived, kissed you and sat down next to you. I felt so bad that I left quickly. I cried loudly, my legs were dry, my hands were shaking and I could not breathe. Hiva took my hand and said loudly,

"Delsa! Delsa! Wake up baby ..."

I did not feel like I was dreaming at all. Everything seemed perfectly alive and real. I felt the pain with all my being. How could it be a dream?!

Ryan! I'm not feeling well. I'm going through hard times. I know your return will not cure my pain; Distance also torments me in this way. I cannot be with you and I cannot see you with anyone else. You are not with me even in my dreams!

I thought months of reading books and psychotherapy sessions were enough; But I still do not feel well. Now I'm worse off than you can understand. Nothing is in its place. These days, when my schedule and tasks are overdue, I think about you more and I get annoyed.

I remembered the days when you would calm me down whenever I shared my worries with you. I had a plan for my training, you were by my side and you helped me. Today I saw one of the films I had taken from your performance. I wanted to take my hand in the film and take your right hand once more and caress it while you play.

As I listened to the audio file of our eleventh session, I remembered how much we laughed together, how much we joked.

When are those beautiful days over? Ryan, I can no longer stand it. It is very difficult to accept this pain. Very!! You know how much I love to call you like in the past and say my dear! Wherever you are, do not leave me unaware, because if you are not good, both of us are not well. I would like to say that if you feel sad and lonely, don't worry; I am with you. Let me know. I follow you to go to the land of timelessness together; Where we do not need a clock and stay together for as long as we want. I want to call and say my Ryan! My beautiful pianist! Come and shake me and wake me up from this nightmare of these seven months. Say you did not go.

The twenty-fifth letter

I called Hiva today and shared my dream with her. I was afraid that if he found out that after seven months, I was still in a bad mood and I think of you, he would be angry with me or not understand me; But he listened to everything I said and tried to calm me down.

I know that he has also experienced a severe emotional crisis in the past.

I met Arash at a concert last year. He was a professional violinist who played and performed on glamorous stages with famous singers. Hiva was fascinated by Arash's situation, not Arash himself. She thought that if they were together, she would become famous and prosper by his side. That is why she considered Arash much higher than herself and did not have enough self-confidence to talk to him;

She constantly tolerated his ugly behaviors. Until one day she decided to end everything with all its pain because she came to the conclusion that she was in a relationship based on her needs and complexes; Not out of love.

Hiva, like me, has been rebuilding herself for months, looking for new meanings for life.

I'm glad I finally got out of the cocoon of my mind and shared my feelings with my closest friend. I needed a compatriot. Hiva was the one who tried to understand and accompany me from the very beginning without any judgment. Not only did she not reject me but she always tried to make me feel better.

Of course, I do not want to put the responsibility for digesting my sorrows on someone else by grieving. I know that even if my best friends are with me, I am still alone in my journey of healing.

No one but myself can properly understand what is going on inside me. Even my therapist cannot make a decision for me and write a prescription for my suffering, because every word of my language in the other mind means with the context of her own life.

What knots have not been opened in me yet that I cannot accept the reality?! Why does your distance still bother me?

The old word nostalgia cannot carry the heavy burden of my feelings. I sometimes feel nostalgia like a pressure on my heart or hatred in my throat. I stand on the ruins of your presence and breathe your memory. I wish you had a picture, a text, a sentence of something from me, in your mind that whenever you think about it, you smile for a few seconds and say how much I loved you!!

If I know that there is a good memory with which you remember me, I will no longer consider my love fruitless ...

Tell me! With what memory do you remember me?!

Conversations with my inner child

"Little Delsa, tell me how do you feel?"

"I'm afraid of the future. I'm afraid I will not be able to do all this. There is no one to help me. I'm alone. If it was Ryan, we would have done all this together."

"That is, instead of us, could he do your exam?"

"No. But he could reduce the stress of the exam. Remember how calm I was on the night of the exam when I saw him?! If Ryan was here now, he would tell me not to worry, it would be okay. In that one sentence, he had so much energy that everything was going well. If it was Ryan, he would work with me and encourage me, I would go with the music and plan with him, and I could play an instrument like that. I'm so confused now that I do not know how to decide! He is not here to tell me what to do. I need Ryan to succeed and achieve my dreams."

"My little Delsa! From now on, I will pay more attention to you on the night of the exam, and I promise to calm you down myself. Whatever grade you get, I love you again and I'm proud of you. We do our best and study seriously. At the end of the exam, we stand together and take the exam together."

"There are so many language teachers. We choose one and move forward regularly. We can also get help from Roya, who has a good language and speak English with each other. There are also so many music teachers, my dear. We commit ourselves to practice at certain times of the day. So, we don't need Ryan anymore. Love cannot solve all our problems. You think you will not feel pain with love and all your pain will disappear; But remember, as long as I live, problems never end, they just change shape. It is our duty to take responsibility for our lives and work and not to blame others. It is our duty to achieve our goals. I do not see you cry anymore!"

"How good I was, you talked to me. I am not alone anymore when I feel like it."

"I will never let you feel lonely again. I am like a shadow with you. Even if it is not sunny and the path is full of darkness, I will be the light that you are not afraid of anything and continue. People come and go; But I always pay attention to you and take care of you. You are my child and I am responsible for taking care of your needs and feelings. Don't expect this from anyone but myself. Now wipe your tears, my dear. I'm by your side. Don't cry anymore."

The twenty-sixth letter

So far, I have gone through several psychotherapy sessions and participated in several webinars on love and relationships.

I have learned that everything that bothers me about others is traits within me that I have suppressed and have not yet come to terms with.

"The traits that bother us in others are the reflection of parts of ourselves," said Carl Jung.

The selfishness of others always bothered me, while my own existence was full of selfishness. Every person who came into my life was a mirror to show myself.

I thought my love was free of selfishness. I was so involved in blaming others and playing the role of the victim that I did not get a chance to see my selfishness. I tried to look at the phenomenon of falling in love with a better perspective. I had to analyze my past patterns.

Talking to my psychiatrist and reading various articles, I found that our subconscious stores many of the movies we watch, the novels we read, and the stories we hear as part of itself, forming a pattern of love to show it to a particular person one day. Perhaps the first glance that could create an emotional bond in our hearts is actually a link to our past; The past may have been wrong.

My mythical idea of love was shaped by what I saw in my childhood animations and romantic movies.

I thought we must have been hermaphrodites one day and we were so strong that Zeus had to separate us. I fell in love with someone who filled my void. Someone who lived my dreams and unlived life.

I wanted you to make my dreams come true. I wanted to complete my ignorance with you. I saw my growth and development only with you. Because I thought you were the lost half of me that we were going to complete together.

I recently read the book "On Love" by Stendha[1], who wrote:

"The crystal coating hides the imperfections or ordinariness of the beloved and makes him different from all other human beings in the eyes of the lover."

I just realized that I had covered your real character with a crystal cover.

Maybe I was in love with someone like you who plays on stage. My dream man was like a beautiful dress that was not your size, and I wanted to force it on you out of selfishness.

I thought I could gradually convince you to immigrate to the United States with my family first, and after a while to go to Vienna together, build a dream life together, tour the world, and travel from country to country.

To think that we cannot live without a particular person means that we are helpless and that helplessness is another form of selfishness.

I was always looking to change you. I was trying to make you a loving, kind, loyal and supportive person. I do not blame you. The problem was that we were

---

[1] Stendha: Nineteenth-century French writer

not on the same level emotionally and did not fit in at all.

Loving is not enough to build and maintain a relationship. It does not necessarily lead to compatibility. Sometimes we become interested in someone whose life goals are not in line with our goals and whose values and worldview are completely at odds with our values and worldview. We should not sacrifice our self-esteem, body and mind and label it as love. In the pleasant song of life, the note of love is important and vital, but not all notes. This song needs more notes to complete. One should not rejoice in love because no kiss has ever signed an engagement note.

I know that religion belonged to your parents, not your choice. Despite having a religious family, you decided to become independent and choose a new lifestyle for yourself.

We needed common values, criteria and ideals to be together. At that time, my expectations were unrealistic. You were "you" and I just realize this. No one can be changed by force unless it is a personal choice and he wants to change. People will not be happy until they do something of their own free will, and if they are not happy, they will not be able to pay the price for an imposed choice. You were looking for other things and I did not want to accept. Instead of taking responsibility for my feelings, I did my best to change you ...

A few days ago, I read a quote from Jorge Luis Borges[1] that struck me:

"You should cultivate your garden instead of waiting for someone to bring you flowers."

My dear Ryan!

I know that no handsome prince is going to come with his white horse and make me happy; Love and happiness are things I have to strive for myself and I should not expect that from anyone else. I should not look for someone who is emotionally higher than me.

I conclude this letter with some beautiful quotes from Mark Manson:

"You need more than love in life. Love is great, love is necessary, But love is not enough."

---

[1] Jorge Luis Borges: Twentieth Century Writer, Poet and Writer

The twenty-seventh letter

My old love!

From the day I tasted your arms until the moment I write this letter to you, I have not touched any man. I did not commit to anyone. I lived with you in the house of my heart and I did not let anyone come inside.

Can you believe me if I say that I am still waiting for the call on Saturday afternoons to arrange our class time?! It seems that somewhere in my heart is still waiting for you. I know that my relationship with you was a combination of images and dreams that had nothing to do with you. I attributed to you, things that were my own achievement. I know all this, but it's harder to accept the reality than I thought.

Today in the poisoned cyberspace, I saw you next to a girl who looked exactly like the one I had in my dream. A girl with long brown hair, black eyes, white and pearly teeth, and light makeup ... I think she was beautiful. I'm glad you found the one you were looking for. Someone who does not have my limits and red lines. I congratulate.

I just have a few small questions! Does that mean your eyes are full of meaning for her, too? Does she worship the parts of your face one by one? Does she tell you poetry? Does she put a photo of your artist's hands in the background of her cell phone? From the audio files you send her, she creates a personal channel and listens to them every night instead of the song. Does she know your voice is stronger than any other painkiller and relieves her fever and headache by listening to pleasant music? Always flexible and apologizing? When you get sick, does she get so upset that she gets sick herself? If she is ill, does she first pray for you to be well?

What do these things really matter? Oh, baby!

Maybe the note of love is not in the range of my voice. Because whenever I wanted to read it, it was not tuned.

I do not own anyone in this world; I realized this the day someone I loved left me and I could not stop him. I could not do anything. I am alone. Even in the arms of my dearest.

The feeling of emptiness has come to me again and it bothers me a lot, but on the other hand, my sense of responsibility does not allow me to commit suicide or harm myself. It may be a little strange that you both love yourself and know that you are responsible for your life, and you do not have any convincing meaning to continue your life, but you are looking for it in your heart.

Love is in a bad mood. It is like a person who has failed in two steps of victory, like falling from the highest precipice in the world, like a happy song; But short very short.

I am sitting by the fireplace, flipping through the book of "Forough" and one by one I find the words of my heart among her poems:

"By God, it is not in my heart and soul,

nothing but regret to see him,

I burned with grief, and who,

my grief is bothering him,

All night in the heart of this bed,

My soul seeks the lost,

From all this fruitless effort,

The confused mind tells me,

The one you are looking for,

Never cares about you,

Stop this moaning,

Stop it, he has another friend,

Candle, candle, what are you laughing at?

 I swear to the dark night,

By God, I died from this regret,

Why not he is in my arms."

Conversations with my inner child:

"Delsa, I miss him very much, very much. I miss his beautiful laughs. His loving eyes. Warm hands. I cannot think of him. I cannot love anyone but him."

"My beautiful girl; I know how much you loved him, but whether you like it or not, this is the truth. Ryan is no more and he is with someone else now. That photo must have made you so bad. We have to give ourselves time. Everything will be fine."

"What has been done so far, Delsa? We are alone. The world is too big and we are too small for it.

Everything is over. We're going to die ... Ryan will never return."

"Do you think we will be immortal if Ryan returns? Will loneliness disappear and we rule the world?"

"I would like to be in his arms if I am going to die one day; Not like this anymore. Death is neither painful nor scary!"

"You are afraid of loneliness and death! Why did I not understand until now?! That's why you cannot cope with separation. Maybe the great anxiety you have about death has caused you to be overly afraid of rejection, to be constantly dependent on others, and to worry about losing them! Maybe thinking about Ryan is your defense mechanism to reduce your anxiety! I'm not saying that this could be all the reason, but I guess a lot of obsessions are related to your inner anxieties!"

"Yes, maybe you are right. I'm scared to death, and this is the first time I'm confessed. I'm afraid of being forgotten. I am afraid of rejection, loneliness, separation and nothingness; But when Ryan was in our lives, he would not let me think about these things. I had forgotten all my worries. I want to go back so I don't have to face my fears. I can no longer bear all this pain."

"Little Delsa! I learned from books that awareness is a condition for entering the path of healing. In the words of Rachel Hallis: "The first step to solving a problem is to admit to having it." You never said you were afraid of death. Maybe from now on we can find the root of many of our fears and problems and do something with a more open mind. The first step we must take to reduce our anxiety is to accept them, and in order to be able to reach this acceptance, we must understand their gift. From now on, we will read more books and meditate. I'm here with you and I'm not taking my eyes off you ..."

The twenty-eighth letter

Dear Ryan!

I am writing this letter under the influence of my psychotherapeutic statements and the book "When Nietzsche Wept.[1]" I like to write down and memorize what I have learned that is valuable.

First of all, in my mind, I removed all my fears and problems in the form of a big sad giant and left it on the ground and imagined that I was sitting on Mars and looking at my problems from that distance.

At the heart of the ever-expanding universe is a planet suspended in space that is as small as a grain of dust against the vastness of the universe. Eight billion people live on it, and each of them is busy.

---

[1] By existentialist psychiatrist and psychoanalyst and American author Irvin Yalom

One corner of it is a girl who has not reached her love and now thinks the world is over.

I no longer saw myself helpless. That black giant, in all its grandeur, was no longer visible and had lost its importance.

Nietzsche was right:

"If we climb high enough, we will reach a height where calamity no longer appears calamity."

Dear Ryan!

Every time I write about my feelings, I travel to deeper layers of my being. This time I realized how scared I am of loneliness and death! This awareness lifted a heavy emotional burden from my shoulders.

There are always signs of death in our daily lives; Such as graduation, dismissal, retirement, immigration, divorce, and the end of an emotional relationship. All of this is a kind of reminder of death and nothingness on a smaller scale, reminding us that life is transient and mortal.

Separation from you was an overnight death that reminded me of a greater death. My great anxiety about death had turned into a fear of loss, and I had not noticed it all these years.

In our subconscious, we seek defensive mechanisms to overcome our existential anxieties! Love is perhaps the most powerful of them all.

We fall in love to end our isolation; Find life meaningful and deny death by living in one's hearts. We fall in love to feel better about ourselves, to lessen the cruelty of the world with attractive fantasies of love, and to relieve the pain of our existential anxieties.

I wanted you to be by my side and always show me the way to achieve my dreams so that I would suffer less by relying on and entrusting the responsibility of my choices. I was experiencing timelessness with you; It is as if I have overcome time. Your love protected me from death and oblivion after death. Your presence filled the place of all the people who were not there and gave meaning to all my work.

I needed you to be my two watching eyes. My life became meaningful before your eyes. Everything I did I had to show to feel like I did it. I attributed these meanings to you myself. You were not responsible for my existential fears.

Nietzsche told Brewer,

"You think of Bertha because you do not want to think about the more important things."

Since facing the facts of life is anxious, I also thought about you so that I would not get involved in this anxiety, and so that I would not think about you, I would warm my head with various things.

We become obsessed with not thinking about the important issues of life, and we create a lot of worries for ourselves to avoid thoughts and fantasies.

We are all murderers!

The murderer of our precious moments. By drowning in past memories and extreme fantasies about the future, we kill our precious present with our own hands. Maybe with this mechanism, we can reduce our anxiety a little, but not for free. By killing our moments, we will have a life without living. If we think that we have a lot of time and transfer some of our opportunities and responsibilities to another world, we may regret it, and the more we regret it, the more we will fear death.

I try to understand myself. Who is not afraid of nothingness and forgetting?! A healthy person must be afraid of death in order to be able to live a genuine life with the awareness of it.

I think there is something deep inside people that longs for immortality and makes them write, read, play, invent and explore and record. Perhaps the creation of many of the books, movies, plays, songs, and sculptures that have survived today is due to the knowledge of death. This is admirable to go to war with forgetfulness and absurdity. How good it is to try to do something before our opportunities run out.

I have fallen in love with Nietzsche's theory of the world forever:

"What is eternal is this life and this moment. This moment will be forever and you alone are your only listener. Life should not be modified or destroyed with the promise of another life in the future. Live in such a way that you fall in love with such thoughts."

The twenty-ninth letter

Dear Ryan!

I would like to write to you about what I have learned and share my good feelings with you.

These days I meditate to calm my body and soul to reduce my stress, increase my concentration and be able to become more aware of my presence at the moment.

Being in the moment does not always mean enjoying, it is important to feel and understand every feeling we have at the moment.

I tried to feel the pain of my nostalgia without denying and pretending to be a false positive; Nevertheless, I found many things in the present moment that I could enjoy and be thankful for. Like watching my favorite movie with a cup of tea and a slice of cake with my dear family, walking in the park with my mom, cooking my dad's favorite food, explaining math problems to my younger sister, playing with my artist friends, listening to my favorite podcast, reading books that help me get better, watching the sunset, seeing the moon and beautiful constellations in the night sky and much more ...

I tried to focus on the sights, the sounds and the smells and to feel the best moment with my eyes, ears, skin, nose and tongue. The most valuable asset of my life is my being with the pure pieces of my being I can see the beautiful face of life, hear its voice, inhale its fragrance, taste it and embrace its moments.

I do not want the day to come when I feel like I did not live at all. Why spend my limited time hating and chewing on past events? Why should I not learn from them and let them go? I have more important things to do. I cannot please everyone. I cannot oppose all the tastes and beliefs of others. My time on this planet is limited and not all of my dreams come true; So, with that in mind, I choose my habits and goals carefully and commit to them.

I have to remind myself every day that life is a precious gift that will one day be taken away from me. Life is too short to wait for someone to come back and change! I want to enter into a new relationship with myself.

With purposeful visualization, I focus my energy on my goals and aspirations and build a house in my mind where my "superior self" is supposed to live.

Before that I had to learn some lessons. First of all, I have to admit that all people leave the planet alone, just as they set foot on it. By accepting it, I will no longer pay a ransom to stay with anyone and I will not damage my self-esteem.

It is the ability to be separate that gives me the right to be myself in my relationships. I can disagree with another person, if necessary, express my anger without fear of losing him or her, and ask for what I want; Because I have not lost myself in anyone's needs and expectations.

"No relationship can end loneliness. Each of us is alone in existence, but we can share our loneliness with together."

Says Irvin Yalom.

He believes that people should accept their loneliness and use it as a form of love and friendship in order to have a genuine relationship with each other.

The path of life is like a train that takes us to a common station. It is true that the destination of all of us is the same, but the path each of us is unique. Everyone rides their own train. We cannot ride the train of our loved ones; We can only move close to the lines.

Another thing I had to learn was to face reality and accept it. I have not thought about suicide since I realized I was responsible for myself and my life. I am the only owner of my own life; Although I did not have the authority to shape different parts of my life, I am responsible for it. I'm a train driver who has to get to the station.

Now I am trying to increase my capacity to love. It is true that I cannot control the love of another person, but I can increase my capacity to forgive and receive love.

The relationship I like is love, respect, kindness and trust, not a momentary and unstable tension. One-sided love is an emotional self-harm. I want someone to both invest in a relationship; Not by dreaming, to be a part of life while we are the most important person in life. Let's not limit each other and recognize our individuality, respect each other's values and red lines, have realistic expectations, and also increase the capacity to accept and tolerate our problems and be with each other.

When I was confronted with a great contradiction between reality and my mental fantasies, I suffered a lot; But with all the hardships it had, I was finally able to feel the pain of reality and no longer deceive myself with my mental painkillers; Because I realized that these seemingly sweet painkillers were wasting my precious opportunities and life.

Mark Manson writes:

"It is not enduring trauma that makes you stronger,

 but the effort you put into pursuing trauma

 that empowers you."

All the people who came into my life were trying to make me understand that I should not rely on relationships for love and happiness; Rather, I must seek them within myself, believe in my abilities, and commit to my goals.

How much warmer and happier the tea of our lives would be if we drank it with the people we loved; But if for any reason they could not or did not want to accompany us, it is our duty to let them go and to maintain our inner happiness, self-esteem and love, and to continue on our path with confidence.

We can love someone deeply without wanting to.

If we truly love someone, we will actively pay attention to their life and growth, respect their constructed world and desire their happiness, and if they do not see happiness with us, it is our responsibility to leave their lives and have the opportunity to love and be loved without any hesitation.

As if we have not gone into darkness, we do not understand light. I am indebted to all those who left me in difficult circumstances to prove to me that I am enough to reach my destination.

The thirtieth letter

Dear Ryan!

Tonight, is your birthday night. I haven't seen you for almost a year! I, who thought I would die one day without you, endured a year away; I survived and continued.

I went through hard days. Although the horrific incident of your departure imposed a lot of pain and pressure on my heart, it gave me the opportunity to travel to my inner dimensions and face myself. Not only did I not lose anything, I gained a lot.

I was so caught up in the swamp of dependence that I could not move. It was after your separation from you that my soul was released from captivity and flew away.

When our relationship ended, I had a unique opportunity to rebuild myself and move forward. I achieved something better than what you could owe me; Commitment to myself and my dreams!

Forgive me! I never saw you as you were.

You had desires in the world that I did not prioritize in my own world. Each of us had our own world.

We could not fill our loneliness with the difference in our attitudes and lifestyles. We both had unique experiences and backgrounds and lived with different values. None of us can judge the other one.

We had to get to know each other to understand each other's worlds and both of us could move toward our own destinies. None of us has failed.

Meeting you was the beginning of a new worldview. You did not come to be the meaning of my life, you came to help me find it.

For a year, I kept spinning and spinning in a whirlpool of rejection until I was able to rise again by accepting reality with all parts of my being and feel the presence of love more than ever in my life.

I found God within myself and I found the love I was looking for. Each piece of the love of my being encourages me to discover another world and opens a new window to my eyes.

I'm excited to know that there is always something waiting for me to do. The meaning of my life is in the hundreds of books I have not yet read. It is among the words of a pure poem that I have not yet written; I have not traveled on many long journeys. It lies in the hidden layers inside me that I have not yet discovered ...

I did my best for this relationship and I have no regrets anymore. I told you that I would rather regret what I did than regret what I did not do. I love every note I played in the step of loving you and I do not regret at all the feeling I had for you.

I'm very happy to meet you and if time went back, I would not have prevented anything from happening. I would go to Pedal Cafe again and spend all those moments, days and months with you to get to where I am now. You were my best teacher. The best person who could teach me the lesson of being strong.

I know there are people who have problems much worse than mine, but life, no matter how hard and bitter, is still worth living. At the heart of all the wounds and sufferings of our lives lies a meaning from which everyone must find something to grow.

"There is nothing that can save a person from the worst of circumstances, as much as knowing the meaning of life,"

Said Victor Frankl.

We are the creators of our lives, and our existence is still valuable no matter what we have lost so far.

Life is like a beautiful song to me with happy and sad chords and loneliness is like silence on the notes. Just as silence is an opportunity to understand previous notes, separation and loneliness can also help you understand the meaning of life and meditate on it so that a person can find her superior self and play the rhythm of her life more gloriously. Everyone is responsible for playing the song of their lives. Some parts of this song may not have been made to his liking, but the responsibility for how he performed it lies with him. Not all events that happen to us may be our choice, but it is always up to us to choose the type of encounter with the events.

Because I'm not perfect, I sometimes make mistakes; I also have many fears in life, but as soon as I accept them and take a step towards improving my negative feelings every day. I rebuild my being with goals, aspirations, acceptance of truths, and the capacity for love, and I strive to become my best self in any situation.

I focus on my physical and mental activities, I write down my memories and feelings, I eat a healthy diet, I get a good night's sleep, I plan my daily routine, I continue to exercise purposefully, I read books, I cook; I participate in different periods of personal development, poetry and music, and every day I meet new people and learn a lot from them. I also try to eliminate my bad habits as much as I can and replace them with good ones.

Dear Ryan!

I like to rewrite our story in my own emotional way. I would like to thank you for the gift I received last year.

There is no expectation behind this small gift. I do not want you to come back; I do this for my own comfort and to make it easier for you to forgive.

"Forgiveness" is a sign of strength, perfection and survival. Nothing and no one can destroy the love that is in this little gift.

I learned to love from Nietzsche, who told Brewer,

"Only when one can live like a hawk, without the need for the presence of another, will one be able to love."

I also learned from Wayne Dyer that

"Love means being able and willing to let those who matter to us choose what they want without insisting that their choice satisfy us."

I love you and respect your choice.

I love you for the good lessons you taught me, the memories you etched in my mind, the songs we played together and the moments we recorded together.

Your love naked my soul so that I could see my wounds better. It made me travel deep inside. It helped me reconsider my past beliefs and behaviors.

I forgive you for myself; Because forgiveness removes the mirror of my heart from turbidity.

One of the most important lessons I had to learn was to learn that leaving is as important as staying. As much as you are, beloved, dear, and respected. By insisting that you want to stay, you are harassing yourself and hurting someone else. You have to let go of the rotten ropes of dependence and leave wherever it's time without insisting on staying.

What beautiful Hussein Vahdani[1] writes in his book
"L of Love":

"He who considers the relationship valuable

also keeps its account well.

Remind me to write to you,

 love should be saved without reckoning,

 but it should be spent with reckoning.

 Love has its own limits.

It depends on your capacity,

 your self-esteem, your dignity, and your personality.

To love that should not make you disrespectful

 and impersonal; Should it?"

I loved you so much that I forgave you and had no
grudge or anger, and I loved myself so much that I
could not wait for you anymore.

I am responsible for my well-being and I have a duty
to take care of myself against injuries. I do not want
to be disappointed anymore.

---

[1] Writer and journalist

I accept the truth with all my pain, and I admit that sometimes I miss you deeply, but every time I miss you, I remind myself of the issues that separated us and refocus on my work.

I would rather be away from you and miss you than feel more homesick next to you. When I cannot squeeze your hands, caress your face, put a kiss on your cheek, write through your eyes and share my love with you, so it's better to stay away from you. Sometimes getting upset is another kind of loving. I love you without waiting. Life without you is going on for me, too.

All our memories, good or bad, are immortalized in these letters, they breathe in our hearts and minds and will be repeated forever. I'm sorry if one of my letters offended you. To calm my heart and soul, I had to put all my words on paper.

I made a beautiful wish for you tonight and hung it on the stars so that the first-night breeze would blow in your hand. Do not forget to raise your hand to the sky tonight.

One of my wishes is your heart's wish, which you wish for every year on your birthday night. I wish we could grow so high and soar in the sky of our dreams that we would both shake hands from afar.

I want you to be happy.

Always laugh my handsome Ryan.

I forgive you for the rain of words on the ground of my song.

I forgive you for the soothing music of the rain in my nostalgic season.

I forgive you for the pleasant resonance of my instrument when the song of remembrance is playing.

Welcome to Earth, my favorite artist! Your old friend

Delsa

A letter to myself

My beautiful heart!

We have gone through difficult days and we will have more difficult days ahead.

Thank you for all the moments you did not give up and for accompanying me with courage and perseverance. You were the only companion on my dark and hard days. From the heart of darkness, I found light and followed you. I realized that all these years I had to travel inside myself and lose a lot of things to get you. I know you and I fall in love with you.

It took me many days to realize the true love of my life, you are the only one I own, the only one who can make my dreams come true and make me happy.

I like this quote from Elif Shakaf[1] in the book "Nation of Love", who writes:

"For all of us, life is a string of births and deaths. Beginnings and endings. To be born at any moment, he must die the moment before. "As for my new birth, the old one must wither and dry."

My dear! Never blame yourself; You were in the moment you could have been. You did your best. I will not allow anyone to disappoint or annoy you anymore. You are a valuable being. Whether you are with someone or not. I will not exchange you for anything else in the world.

I will always love you and be proud of you. Your constant companion

Delsa

---

[1] Elif Shafak: Turkish-English writer

I love you…

Pedal Café was still a warm and lovable café for me.
A year after I went there, all my beautiful memories
came alive. How I missed the lemon tea.

Ryan was very happy to see me. He looked at me
dumbfounded and asked with his eyes what I was
doing there. Every few minutes we look at each
other. I was not thinking about the past or the future.
I tried with all my being to be present at that time
and to enjoy the present as much as I could.

I asked, "You still play the piano well."

"How are you, Delsa? What are you doing here?"

"I had to give you something. I came to give you.
You better decide for yourself what you want to do
with it."

"What is this? .... Oh ... thank you dear ... thank you for keeping it for me."

"Happy Birthday, Ryan."

"I really thank you. Very kind of you."

I said, "I always wanted to have a good picture of each other. I was sick of the last words for months and I was upset that I was angry with you."

Ryan: "I apologize to you."

Me: "Even though I have already forgiven you; these words were very valuable to me."

Ryan: "Believe me, I remembered you very much. I wanted to talk to you. You are very dear to me. You know yourself. At that time, we had to separate. I did not want you to be bothered anymore."

I said, "I do not approve of your work, but I understand. Our relationship that day was very toxic. It had to be finished. Our mistake was that we did not specify the task of our relationship earlier and we were lost. Otherwise, you would not be a bad person."

I continue with confidence, "During this year that I was away from you, I realized that love is not really dependence and selfishness. I was always waiting for our relationship to become serious. I had set my energy on something that had no external existence. But little by little, I learned to take responsibility for my own life. When I saw that we could not divide our loneliness together, I decided instead of focusing all my energy on one image and imaginary mentality, to put the same energy into the growth of my character, on the work I like to do and to create a new meaning for my life again. And move in that direction."

"How much your tone has changed, Delsa. You have grown a lot in this one year. I admire you. I hope I have had a positive impact on your growth. Whether educational or non-educational."

"You definitely did."

"Delsa! Many things have changed. I struggled with a serious illness for a month and thought I was going to die. My life has become more meaningful. I do not take myself hard anymore. I want to live a better life."

"Thank God you are fine now. I am very glad you came to this conclusion."

"Now my life has changed and I think we can be together ..."

"But I do not think so, because now for me other things are my priority and my goal is to leave Iran."

"Do you really want to go? What if I ask you to stay? You know I'm more comfortable here. My family, my job, everything is here. It's very difficult for me to start from scratch again."

"I made my decision, Ryan, no one can stop me. If I had been that selfish person before, I would have insisted that you come with me now, but because your comfort and happiness are important to me, I would let you choose what you like. I hope your life has changed to become your best self. I ask God to put the best in the path of your life."

"If I had any doubts so far, now I am sure that the separation was in the interest of both of us. Now that you want to go, you can no longer even think about our relationship. But this is without the fact that I have always loved you and never wanted to hurt you. I hope you get what you want. Hope to see you."

"Ryan! This is my thirtieth visit and I am very happy for today and this moment. Thank you for everything. Hope to see you."

"I love you."

"I love you too..."

The sweetness of our footsteps in that dark alley next to the cafe erased the bitterness of the last memory from my mind.

The image of his leaving was blurred in the frame of my eyes. Brewer cried when he realized he had to forget Bertha. According to him, it was very difficult to ignore that image, that magic.

We have never seen each other since. Whatever it was, bitter or sweet, it passed. I do not think I need these letters anymore. I have to lighten my load as much as I can from the past so that there is room for more important things. Tonight, I will burn all these letters and say goodbye to my favorite artist. This relationship has taught me valuable lessons that I will never forget.

Whether I am happy or sad, the earth continues to spin, the sun rises, the moon rises, the flowers bloom, the blossoms bear fruit, the world clock does not stop, the asphalt of no street destroys because of my tears, the world is indifferent to me, it works. I am the only one who can be my savior and supporter.

It is true that I am very small, but in my own world, I have countless meanings, big and small, that I can find by living in the moment.

I was so lucky to set foot on this planet as a human being to enjoy life's journey. To be able to enjoy breathing, eating, drinking, sleeping, and traveling, to feel, to fall in love, to forgive, to choose, to have aspirations and goals, to read, write, play, and create.

I'm glad to see the end of my twenty-four years. Tonight, I wish to take stronger steps toward my dreams. Be happier and stronger than before and be able to help others.

In this infinite world, the probability of me being born was very small; But I was given this unique opportunity. It is true that I borrowed life from existence and one day I have to repay it with death, but this valuable loan is not given to everyone. Everything has a price. In return for the great grace that has been bestowed upon me, I will pay the price of becoming a human being by overcoming my sufferings. By living well, I prove to the universe that I deserve to be born and live, and that I make the most of the limited time I have been given and appreciate it.

I feel proud of the lover I loved with all my being, heroically endured his sufferings and hardships.

My life is a glorious journey of love, on the path of learning and growth, and this journey continues as long as I live.

I look forward to meeting new people. I'm ready to fall in love again. I want to invite my inner love to the outside and not be afraid of anything; Because I'm still breathing.

Happy Birthday to me...

Darya Mohammadi was born on 1998.

She is a young author, musician, lyricist, narrator, and piano instructor. She holds a bachelor's degree in biology from Beheshti University.

In the fall of 2021, the book addressed to my beloved artist was published in Iran for the first time, and in the summer of 2022, the second edition was published. Now in 2023, this book is published internationally in English & Farsi Edition.

To Access Persian Edition please hit this code:

How to Access Kidsocado Publishing House

www.ingramcontent.com/pod-product-compliance
Lightning Source LLC
Chambersburg PA
CBHW011039190726

48290CB00011B/2926